You Made Me This Way
The Life of Bobby D.

A Novel by
Melissa Cobb

Statement

Wherefore I praised the dead which are already dead more than the living which are yet alive. (Ecclesiastes 4:2)

Chapter 1

I was sitting next to the back row
in the sanctuary and above the
music, I heard two twenty-year old girls talking.
The tall one said, "He called me
his charcoal, black and thick booty, princess.
Girl, that made
me ride him slower and more pleasingly. Now
you want to talk about taking care of me; he was."

They giggled some as the short
one whispered, "Then what?"
"My toes started going all over the place while
I was biting my lip. I ain't ever had it like that girl;
especially from an older man."

That was all I got a chance to hear as I heard my
mother proudly proclaim, "You dick sucking demon
come out of her, in the name of Jesus!"

I was startled. I realized I was sitting in
church eavesdropping on how one girl was
describing her night with a Deacon in the church;
but she didn't say who. I looked at the altar and
thought I was crazy until I heard it again, "You dick
sucking demon loose her and let her go. I say. You
have no more power or dominion over
her mouth right now! In the name of Jesus come
out!"

My ears deceived me not. I heard it
right. Getting up from my seat, almost everyone had

their eyes closed. The Deacons has the best view of everything; therefore, I made my way towards Hustla. There he was obeying the deliverance team directions about keeping the eyes closed. He was sitting on the back row of the Deacon's area. I sat beside him and bump his elbow. He lifted one eye at me. I closely leaned and whispered, "Did you hear what she called out?"

He opened his eye wider and whispered back, "Yeah" as he turned his head back straight and closed his eyes again.

Moving closer towards him I said even quieter than I first spoke, "You don't think that's odd?"

He did not open his eyes as he murmured softly with his lips, "No."

With a cunning grin I stated teasingly, "Hustla, she said dick sucking demon in church."

This time when he spoke "And?" he opened his eyes with a question as if it was ok.

"You know that ain't right" I stated to him. Hustla whispered, "I saw you eavesdropping on those girls and not having your eyes closed; now tell me was that right?"
I gave a slight chuckle because his eyes must not have been closed for him to see what I was doing. However, it bothered no one else but me

about the demon she was conjuring up. She could
have used a better name like Spirit of Oral Sex
or Spirit of Premarital Sex but dick sucking
demon? Then again, I'm twenty-one and could be
wrong. She is the preacher and I am not.
Hustla closed his eyes and bowed his head back
down. I bowed my head and leaned
towards Hustla. Somehow, he knew my eyes were
not closed; therefore, he turned his head towards me
and squinted his eyes tighter for me to copy him.

My cousin Hustla is one of the best. His
mother was married to my dad's brother, and she
died. His father, to my knowledge has never let him
forget it. My uncle became a drunk and cared not
about his only child. I don't really know how it all
came about but we took him into our home when he
was about seven and I was two. The weight of
feeling like you are the reason your mother is not
here can do something to a person. It should have
broken you down, but it didn't do that to Hustla.

He took a hold to the Word of God seriously
and never looked
back. He has always been a perfect role model
and the good boy who never disobeyed my
parents. Hustla is like the brother I never had and
the child my parents have always wanted. You
could talk to my cousin about anything and he
would give an unbiased opinion. You may not like
his answers but he will be fair; however, I became

3

the complete opposite. Yes, I rebelled. I got tired of hearing how God has a call on my life and I don't even know what that call is. I got frustrated about people dictating how I should live or what I should do when they themselves are not even close to living right.

I heard my mother screaming, "Open your mouth wide and let that dick demon out! Let that dick sucking demon out right now in the name of Jesus!"

Tilting my head forward my eyes quenched closed. I know I am not supposed to be looking but I could not help it. Slowly I opened my eyes. I don't know if I was being nosey or maybe I just had to see what was going on in front of me. The deliverance team members now had Tina in a semicircle; I saw her shaking and jumping in front of momma. I know deliverance is good but parts of me couldn't believe it because every week a new demon is called out of her; like there isn't anyone else to live in.

I closed my eyes and thought *how each demon would be stronger than the last demon from last week. When will these people realize there is no power in this church? I say no power because I know how my mom lives behind closed doors. You supposed to have enough power to change the way you are but my mother doesn't have enough power*

4

to keep from cursing. I opened my eyes and heard a frail, crying and teary-eyed tone declaring, "You can't live here anymore. I don't want you here. Leave me. Leave me alone forever."

I closed my eyes again and thought, *I'm not saying the Lord can't use my mother because HE can. The Lord can use anyone that will let them be used by HIM. The people here at this church, don't believe she is a fake because they don't see what I see. My own father refuses to see her for the demon she really is. I love her but I don't love the way she is misusing God's Word or people. I don't know how I could ever expose her or talk about her? I in some form have tried to warn my mother about being in leadership position and how God will cleanse HIS house first; either she doesn't listen because I am the one telling her or she just doesn't care.*

After all she may not be living or doing right, it still does not mean she is not called to preach God's Word or to deliver God's people. It's not that I hate church I have done it too much coming up. I mostly saw how my mother pimp God's people and it made me sick. Whatever she thought she wanted, they all went out their way to get it. They were really taking care of my mother and her extravagant means. Some have mortgaged their homes, many did fundraisers and the majority gave hundreds of dollars on top of tithes, every week.

I cannot be a part of this heresy any longer, but how can I not? I'm the Undertaker for the family business who lives at home but that shouldn't matter. A few years ago, a man told my parents they will have a great ministry of speaking because she and my dad are fluent with words. Their gift will make you do anything they want in the name of God. Personally, God's gift was used the wrong way; especially by my mother. I even spoke behind the podium about false prophets but the people had deaf ears. I think it is because my mother their pastor did not bring the Word to them she brought the Word at them. I opened my eyes and glanced around this very large church.

However, there are a few members that do enjoy hearing us all speak. The first one is my father Deacon Lee Reed who writes the policies and oversees the family business. He is a push over when it comes to my mother. He knows she can be out of line and out the Will of God. He would tell her but when she pouts and carry on; he shuts down the discussion for her to win. In all honesty, he is not strong enough to lead these people either and who would follow a man that lets his wife lead him?

The second one is my cousin Houston "Hustla" Reed. He happens to be the

Director of the Funeral home my dad owns.
He also organizes funerals and picks up the
bodies at hospitals or anywhere. In early life, he
gave his life to Christ and has not shown me
otherwise; that much I can truly say. He to me is
very seasoned and the people would probably fire
him because he preaches the true Word of
God. Hustla will speak against sin as if it were
God HIMSELF. He would not preach prosperity,
blessing, or any feel-good message unless he's
lead This man of God, doesn't care
how anyone feels about it; he is going to preach
God's Word.

But here at the Reed's Chapel United Love
Ministry they only
hear fortune messages, healing messages, prosperity
messages, giving messages and "we don't preach
about sin around here messages" from my mother.
If they got Hustla to preach the church would be
empty; except for his young wife Inga Shells-Reed
who happens to be the Secretary of this church and
of our funeral home called The Last Word Resting
Place.

When I glanced up I saw my mother being
confident as she stated, "Satan you have no more
claims to her. She has denounced you once and for
all! She does not belong to you. Flee her right now!
She belongs to Jesus Christ!"

As if Tina were under a
silent command, her hands became raised in a
surrender motion with her head tilted back. I saw
her grandmother Mother Clark praising God as
Tina's mouth flew open and
trembled vigorously back and forth as if she
was sucking a dick. The deliverance team lady
rushed to get a sheet, a small bucket and some
napkins. She began spitting up, and choking as she
fell onto the floor rolling as if she was on fire. I
know she can move but for all these people
to witness how she was literally fucking the floor
was phenomenal.
My momma the Minister got on the floor with her
as she was making growling sounds that didn't
sound human or right. I recalled her telling
me, *"Something has to give today. I can't keep
living like this. I have to change Bobby D."* Plenty
of times she comes from church claiming she
doesn't want to do anything anymore. She always
screams how she must change yet; does the same
thing. I assumed this was just like other times and
like always I didn't believe her.
After seeing her act like this with the
deliverance team all around her, I knew this was
the transformation Tina was talking
about earlier. Seconds later, she somehow stood up
and so did momma. Two women held the white
sheet around her while another one placed the

bucket in front of her. I heard momma exclaim, "That's it. Spit it out! Spit out that dick sucking demon out! No more oral sex! No more putting your mouth down there to please men! Let that demon go back to the pits of Hell from where he belongs! In the name of Jesus!"

She was crying and yelling hysterically, "Thank you Jesus. Thank you. Jesus, I'm free! Yes, Lord I am free!"

Momma spoke softly with love, "You are delivered this day. Go and sin no more. Do what you must to stay clean. Not too many people get a chance to come back to Christ after living their way without HIM. HE has blessed you and you are free and not bound. Someone from the church will contact you to further help you in your walk with the Lord."

She gave Tina a hug and everyone clapped. When she turned around, I immediately saw the change. I heard the older married deacon in front of me say quietly in disbelief, "Pastor done called out the wrong thang."

I was surprised as Tina walked back to her seat. The deliverance team picked up the small trash can and went in the back. Momma stood at the podium and spoke, "A powerhouse combination is not a gangster and a hoe and it's not one in church and one out of church. The awesome combination is when two people together serve the Lord. If you are with someone and they are going in an opposite direction than you, it should be time for you to see you are going nowhere fast. If he or she loves you, get married; make it right in the eyesight of God. The Word clearly states, how God honor marriages and how it is better to marry than to burn. Either you like them taking you to Hell or you don't know you're going to Hell. However, you put it you have a ticket that's taking you to the bottomless pit with reservations; if you don't change. I can't stress the importance enough about serving the Lord. The Word says you can't serve two masters. You must know your place in this world because everyone has some type of calling on their lives but this sinful skin won't let you answer the phone to Jesus. People have the mind to do right but their flesh won't let them. Church don't you get it? The conclusion is if you are going to go to Hell, is the person you going to Hell for worth it? Is that person good enough for you to

have an everlasting place in torment and torture? You can only go wrong for so long and then what? What if you lose your grace and die before you can come back to the righteousness in Christ? What are you going to do when you need HIM and HE does not know you? What are you going to do when you die in your mess huh? Just because God can be a forgiving and gracious God doesn't mean HE won't send you to Hell. To be frank with you, HE won't send you; you send you. In general, your choices do. You don't want to die without knowing the Lord Jesus. You don't want to take that big of a chance. I don't care how skilled of a gambler or risk taker you are. Let us all stand so we can be dismissed; if there aren't any announcements."

"There are no announcements" Inga stood up to say.

"Bobby D. dismiss the church" mother stated as she went to the back of the church.

I was really surprised by my mother's words. I stepped onto the side podium and stated, "Raise your hands" and everyone did.

"Repeat after me: Lord, protect us this day and every day as we leave your presence and not your sight. Keep us until we all meet again. Amen."

After everyone said that I stated, "Now turn and hug someone you hadn't hug before. We are dismissed in Jesus name."

While everyone was hugging and chatting, I went in the back and help do the days counting. When I approached my mom's study I knew she was back to her old self. Even with the door closed I knew it was something very upsetting because she spoke about Hell; which was new but I heard her yell out, "Reed is written on the door of this

building and this is **my** damn building. By
that what **I** say goes! **Y'all** may pay the cost but **I**
am the boss and **I** run this here fucking
church. **I** won't let **any of you** tell **me** what the
world to do!"

I knew someone had said or did something
they shouldn't have. I opened the door and saw how
they all seemed somewhat stunned to hear her curse
but not me. Mother Clarke stated, "Everybody give
the Pastor some room. The Lord just used her to
deliver a powerful demon, out of Tina."

Momma seemed tired as she said, "I apologize
for my outbursts so don't act like any of you have
never been angry before. That demon in that gal has
worn me out and you all came in here before I can
unwind."

No one said a word as my mother stated her
claim. Mother Clarke spoke up, "The Pastor is right.
We all have said things out of context and the Lord
has forgiven us so we are good. Let us leave out and
give her space."

I have heard her slip of the tongue more than
they think and her "slip of the tongue" is her natural
way of speaking. When everyone began to clear out,
my mother said, "Bobby D. you stay here. I
need a word with you."

They all left me alone with my mom. I cared
not to be in the ministry but she claims God told her

I am to preach HIS Word. I beg to differ. I don't
think HE has called me any more than she
thinks HE has called her but that's my own
opinion. When the last person left out the door,
mother quickly went in her wine cabinet. She was
acting like an alcoholic; trembling and in tuned to
what she was doing. Mother poured herself a tall
glass of Brandy with crushed ice
from study fridge. I stood there and watched her
savor the taste as it was going down her throat.

I do oppose of her drinking and as usual she
tells me all the time, "Jesus drunk wine." I
politely remind her how Jesus's wine did not have
extra liquor in it and HIS wine was not man made
either. However, it does no good. She does what she
wants because she is the leading Pastor. I was going
to speak but as soon as she removed the glass from
her lips she let out a deep sigh before saying, "After
teaching and leading these bastards all day, all the
time, I need a little something to help me out. There
is no way a preacher can deal with
these fuckers, their problems and keep a sober
mentality. If they do, I guarantee they pop pills or
smoke dope."

"Momma those are your church members.
You are to lead and guide them. These people left
all they knew to follow you but they don't know

you are not leading them as they should direct them."

She snickered as she asked me point blank, "And what does that supposed to mean?

"It means you should lead them to God and how to live an overcoming life. Not say one thing and do another. That is like being unstable in your ways."

"And your point is?"

"How can a faithful church follow a faithless preacher?"

Momma took another swallow, which was longer than the first one. She kind of laughed as she removed the glass from her lips. I didn't know what to think but she said, "They are to do as I say and not as I do. Shit, I make mistakes. They better set their eyes on God and not man because this flesh will fail them every time. That is why I talk to you a lot. You know how to hear and not listen, but your problem is; you're worried about the wrong damn thing."

"What is the wrong thing?"

"You worried about me in my calling. Don't worry about that. Get your own calling together and then don't tell me about it; show me about it. I got me and mine get yours."

"If this is what the call of God is HE can keep it. There is no way I would serve a God that would make me live and act like you."

"If you turn your back on God, that's you. I'm doing what's best for me and only me; damn those members."

"Mom no matter how I keep your secrets, they are still your followers, and their blood will be required on your hands; not mine. I hate seeing you on your way to Hell and taking these people with you. But you already know that don't you mother? I don't have to tell you."

"You are acting like seeing me like this is brand new to you?"

"It's not. I'm just tired of knowing how you really are."
She threw the glass at me. I barely moved out the way as she hissed, "What you eat don't make me shit. All you need to know is I shit, and from the looks of my shit; I been taking care of your shit."

"You can curse and get angry with me all you want Mother. The truth doesn't change; people do. You are no ordinary person you are a demon straight from the pits of Hell with a room waiting just for you."

"I do as the Lord tells me, and your job is to do as I say; not watch me do."

Trying to keep my cool, I lightly stated, "Mother with no disrespect."

"None taken" she swiftly replied.

"All closed eyes aren't sleeping eyes. Some of these people will wake up, realize they are on their way to Hell and it's all because of their beloved Pastor."

"Do you think you can do a better job than I can? You work with the dead; the living is your problem."

"Breathing or not; I know I can do a better job than you" I quickly came back at her.

"Well preach. Let me see what you got" she stated as she got another glass from the cabinet and poured more Brandy.

"Mother I can't do that. I will wait on God for HIM to tell me when my time is; if I have a time. Whichever way, I will not force HIS hand in my life all for proving a point. You are doing exactly what the leaders did back in Jesus time. They wanted HIM to prove who HE was, but HE told them HIS time had not come. The same goes with me; my time has not come."

"The Word says be ready in season and out of season."

I spat back, "Even the devil knows the Word Mother."

She looked at me over the rim of her glass to say, "If I wasn't tipsy, I'll beat you backwards bring you back to me and beat you again."
I did not say a word. I waited for her to finish talking. My mother spoke with clarity, "Get this through your head. Who do you think pays for all the fine things you ever had growing up? Who do you think made it happen for you and that top-notch education, surely not your father that spineless bastard. But I love him. Who do you think keeps a roof over your head? Like it or not, its good money being a preacher, pastor, teacher or whatever. You only speak for what-twenty minutes
on a Sunday and it's a feel-good message at that, teach a bible class for what- an hour during the week and occasionally pray for people. You in there with a set salary for about seventy thousand a year or better; you can't beat that. The members will do whatever you tell them because they know by bringing a person of God a glass of water they are blessed. You find a fool bump its head."

"Mother you are using these people and bumping a whole lot of heads. I don't like it. I am sure the Lord is not pleased with you and how you feed HIS people."

"If I can read, I can feed. What is it, Bobby? Am I that bad of an example you wouldn't want to be an assistant pastor here? You can make a hell of a lot more money than you do right now."

As harsh as I could I spoke with clench teeth, "I wouldn't want to be near your calling when God starts cleaning HIS house."

Mother laughed as she snarled, "You don't think the Lord works through me?"

"I didn't say that because the Lord used an ass before. Why not a two legged one?"

"My only child. You are so funny. Did you not see how I was used to deliver Tina today?"

"I did see the move of God today; that I can't lay."

"My child, it can be tedious at times but rewarding that is why I believe this church is ready for the next step."

"Which is?"

She took a gulp and stated with joy, "For those twenty-one and older to meet me at the Buzzard's Hangout."

"Momma! That is a place where drunks and prostitutes go. You can't seriously be for real."

"Yes, I am. The Buzzard's Hangout is also a place where you can shoot pool, meet new people and have some fun. We will be there in groups on Bible class nights. We want them to understand, if we come to their place and discuss biblical issues; they can come to our church and hear what thus says the Lord. This is a window of opportunity for the church to go in and let them see we are human just like them. We are not perfect, and they should see that."

"Well, I'm not going. You can call me out of line or disobedient all you want. I've had enough of living one way and teaching another."

"That's you. Bobby D. you are twenty-one and can make up your own mind, but I plan on being there and having an exciting time."

"Does daddy know?"

"It doesn't matter if he knows or not. I am the pastor here not him. He can go and see for himself, or he can stay at home like you."

"Momma bad rubs off on good not the other way around."

She didn't say a word as I asked, "Are you even ready for the people to see you with your Brandy?"

"I'm saying it's an opportunity for people to get to know each other. I can drink and I won't get drunk."

I stated with a question on my clear face, "You really believe God is telling you to do these things, don't you?"

"I do and you can't run from your calling no more than jumping off a building can make you fly."

She took a few more swallows of her spirits in a glass as she poured her some more before telling me, "Look every Sunday and every Tuesday, I teach. Many of them call me for this and that and I minister to them what the Word says. Overall I do it very well with no complaints. All I can tell them is what's right and what's wrong. If they don't get if for themselves that's on them. I can and will only do so much. I have my own demons to face; my own problems to deal with. If these eight hundred plus members think I can work a miracle because I fast and pray; the devil is a lie."

"That is when you supposed to be in a place to do such things and have a team of prayer warriors with you doing the same thing."

"Supposed to be and is, are two different things. Ask your father he knows what I am talking about."

"I don't have to ask him. I don't even care to ask him."

"Bobby D. that's your problem right there. We are your parents, and we are in the Lord. You obey us but you don't like us. You aren't close to him and you damn sure ain't close to me."

"Now you mother misleads God's people and I don't like you for it. Father, he allows you to do it and for that I barely tolerate him but between the two; I'll choose him. With that being said, it's best for me to keep my distance and my mouth shut."

My mother did not say another word as she drunk another glass of her demon liquor and sat back in her chair with her eyes closed. My mother is going to Hell and she is taking these not so innocent people with her. They have a bible. They can read and search the scriptures for themselves but they don't in a way. I can't in sense blame them for not knowing how their lovely pastor acts behind closed doors. But one thing I do know is, the devil does not know how to live right.

They should have known something was up when last week my mother was in the pull pit talking about how we all need a little pick me up sex. She even stated how the hand-held microphone reminded her of a hard but sturdy cock. They gasp in amazement but that was all they did. I was the only one who paid attention to it. My mother continued by saying, how she needs it all the time and if her husband doesn't want to get with it, she'll get a toy and have a sex party. They all agreed. I was just stunned at their ignorance.

Hustla didn't like it because I saw it on his face. He knows I will tell her of her errors quicker than he or my dad. On that day, he knew I was about to stop her but he motioned for me to stand down and leave it alone. I had to sit there and listen to her speak on how a good piece of dick will brighten your day and all the women were agreeing. I could only shake my head. I have tried warning them but they don't listen. They think I am unlearned but the truth is, Hustla or myself is more prepared to lead them than my own mother is. Even my dad will give it a better try than what these people are getting right now.

I looked back over at her. She was meditating as I asked, "I am not going to tell dad that you have been drinking but do you need me to let dad know you will be home late again?"

Momma placed her hands behind her head and spoke with her feet resting on anottoman, "No, I'll be right on. I just need a few minutes to gather my thoughts. But regardless of what you think of me, don't let how I do things mislead you from God. HE is always the answer."

"Too late."

I spoke that as momma closed her eyes, I eased out the door. I know she really means she needs to let the Brandy get her mellow before she greets any more people or go home. She is a liar, a drunk and those are to name a few. Soon as I find my own place, I am bouncing like a ball and joining the Elite Sniper Unit. I know the Lord loves me but I must first love me and no one on this earth going to do that for me but me. Trust and believe you must understand from the world's point of view. I just don't think I want any call on my life, if it gets me to doing what my mother does.

I have Jesus in me, but I would rather my flesh rule me. It's just that I don't need her help. I am fine the way I am. I don't bother anyone, and I don't run either. I am not ready for the life of going to church all over again; nevertheless, leading people to a God, I haven't felt myself. I believe I'll be short changing the people and directing them to Hell as I have seen my mother do.

Chapter 2
Eight Years Later

I stood in the living room part as long
as I could; with my bow and arrow on my back and
my nine-millimeter with silencer on my hip. They
are in the room having a grand ole time and not
noticing I have broken into their hotel suite. *Time to
interrupt the party* I thought. When I came in vision
of the bed, the lady had her head under the cover,
and I know what she was doing. Slyly I
grinned because they are going to hate the day I
caught them for my client.
Sadly, enough I will miss this kind of work, but I
feel my time is at an end for private jobs. One thing
I have learned from the military is, how you do
not show any emotions and today I won't. Focusing
on the task at hand, I cleared my throat and turned
the main light switch on. They jumped and she
came from under the covers. I stood there as the
lady seemed fearful and stunned as she
asked, "Who are you?"

Me with my mask on and wearing all
black, I did not answer at first. The man yelled,
"You in the wrong room, buddy!"

He reached for the phone, but his reactions
were slow. Like lightning, I put an arrow through

his hand as it pinned it to the headboard. She was hollering as I said, "Throw the covers on the floor."

Crying some, the woman did as she was told. The man asked in pain, "What do you want?"

"Your money is no good to me."

"I will pay you triple whatever they are paying."

"You can't buy me" I stated with a tease.

"Don't you know who I am? Don't you know the kind of trouble you will be in when I find out who you are?"

"I'm not concerned about the trouble, and I do know exactly who you are. You are the famous Levar Fanning. You inherited some of your millions and you made millions more. You are the CEO of The Southern Baptist Committee and you are legally separated from your wife; who plans to take half if not all your millions. You have done a lot of charitable deeds from hosting Child Abuse Awareness, Cancer Walks, donated houses for the homeless, sponsored Toys for Tots, gave generously to Veterans, and Scholarship's for underprivileged high school seniors. The list goes on and on with your notable deeds but that is all they are; good deeds."

I looked at her and spoke, "Now you all prim and proper married money. You are a gold digger and a wreck waiting to happen. You are the lovely Lisa Grady-Hawkins the wife of Senator Roger Douglas Hawkins. You have three children young children, an upstanding citizen in your community, you're on the PTA, an active member of Booster Club and the worst part is; you all attend the same church. As for me, I am here on a mission."

"How do you know so much about us?" the man asked in pain.

"It's my job to know about the men and women who lie and defile God's marital bed."

"Please don't kill us. We won't see each other again" Lisa begged.

Ignoring her plea, I spoke out loud, "What should I do with you two adulterers?"

"Please let me go home. My family needs me" the woman asked.

"You are going home but you will be a changed woman from this day forward."

I smiled at her a crazy smile, with evil on my mind. I've never had a cheating person to do this, and it would be unorthodox but why not; it's my last private mission. Boldly I stated, "Put his dick back in your mouth."

Mr. Fanning asked, "You want her sucking on me in front of you? What kind of unmoral person are you?"

"Not just suck on you but eat that dick, in front of me."

"I promise I won't suck that dick again. Please don't make me do this" she pleaded with a lot of compassion.

"Don't have to promise me because right here, right now you will bite the head off and swallow the head."

Her face became pale as she looked puzzled. She asked me in a quiet tone, "What did you say?"

Sounding louder, I shouted "You heard me. Bite the head off and chew that dick!"
The guy started begging and pleading as he began to squirm. I kept my eye on her as I pointed the gun at him. Her face was priceless. He spoke, "I've had enough of this! She's not doing anything, but you are leaving."

"She will do what I tell her and right now; she's swallowing dick."

"She said they were divorced" he yelled.

"That's not my business about her lies. Fanning, you should have read the fine print on how cheating doesn't pay."

I stepped back and shouted, "Put your mouth back on him and bite the top off now; before I blow YOUR HEAD off!"

He tried getting up but quickly remembered, the arrow is still in his hand. I shot a blank warning shot. I thought about the scripture having one eye or leg going to heaven then two going to Hell. I stated, "It's better to live with the dick head missing than to die with everything in place, Mr. Fanning."

The unsuspected man did not move as he became very impotent. I stated to the woman, "Make it rise with your mouth like you were doing and pull on it fast. I have another engagement."

This woman was crying and begging as she put her mouth back on him. It appeared how she was just sucking. I screamed, "Start biting."

Mrs. Hawkins started gnawing and pulling on her rich lover. I could literally hear her slurping from where I was standing. He cried out, "Don't make her do this to me. I am a man for God's sake!"

"You are also a cheater who should have thought with his other head."

The cunning woman was taking too long. I pointed the gun at her temple and verbally said, "If you don't bite it, I will kill you first and cut it off myself; either way his dick is going to be headless."

This time she really tried biting it off. The man hollered at the top of his lungs. I didn't get any enjoyment, but it comes along with this type of job. I focused back on the woman as she was doing her best to tear the top of the dick head off. After moments of working her head back and forth with a lot of tugging I heard the muscle tear from his body as the man shook and hollered for dear life.

I removed the gun from her head and moved backwards. This time, when she held her head up, there it was hanging between the clutches of her red stained teeth, a mushroom top with veins, white tissue and blood underneath. He passed out. She really did look like an animal who killed its prey. Her eyes were big, and the woman had a rash breathing about her. She made angry noises and tearful eye piercing stares at me. It was truly disgusting to see blood dripping from her mouth, then onto her chin and breast. She has the pleasure tool hanging under her nose and now no one will ever get it.

The most amazing part is, I came here to do a job, and I perfected it better than I thought. With authority, she heard me say, "Now chew that dick and swallow that head."
Her body became jerking from crying as it told me no; nonverbally. I knew she didn't want to do it, but she had no choice. She chewed as if someone was trying to take the hot piece of meat from her. I could only watch, and she could only stare at me with hate and anger. Leaning forward a little I commanded, "Now open your mouth. I need to make sure it's in your stomach."

The woman opened her mouth wide as she cried. I saw it was gone, and the man was still unconscious. I took my arrow out his hand and left out the room unnoticed the same way I entered. Soon as I arrived at my location, I got a text stating the rest of my money had been wired in the secured location and thanks for doing my job completely. I drove the rental car back to Enterprise and had a driver take me to the airport. I've made up my mind about seeing the top of the world.

As luck would have it, my plane was delayed, which is not good news. I decided on renting a room for the night. I got in a taxi and before I could make it there, my cell phone rung. I thought I was mistaken as I saw the number appear on my ID. I hadn't seen this number in years and suddenly here it is. I paid it no attention and went inside of my hotel, got a room and locked the door. Many things had crossed my mind and why my mother was calling me was one of them. I haven't sent her a birthday card or anything and now she is calling me. It has been years since I saw her and the last time I saw her, we got in a word fight about how she was misleading the people at Reed's Chapel United Love Ministry. I sighed and ignored the call again. I know she will not leave messages because I don't have a voicemail set up. If I want to talk to you or anyone, I would pick up the phone. Me not talking to her should be a sign that I don't want to deal with her. I really don't care what's on her mind. I know I am her only child but that makes no difference; just because she had me.

Now I'm wondering why her? My own dad never called me. Hustla told me once how my dad is waiting until I want to talk about whatever it was that made me leave out the blue. He stands behind her and that is his wife. He should stand behind her but not if she is doing things unlike God; like she was back then. I'm glad I didn't stick around but if I had stayed, I wouldn't have all I have now. Then again if I had stayed, I would probably be a lying preacher or a hypocrite church member.

Closing my mind on my family, I washed off and was about sleep when I heard a tone that made the tiny hair on the back of my neck stand up, *"Nine months."* I opened my eyes and looked around the room. I closed my eyes and attempted to sleep again. This time louder I heard, *"Nine months."* This time, I laid there at first but eventually I sat up and took notice of my quiet hotel room. I slept in the jungle among poisonous snakes, spiders and things. I have been shot at and I have killed but this voice I could not tell if it were male or female.

This time I turned over and closed my eyes. This time the voice was closer. In fact, the words whispered, *"Nine months; a work to do."* This time my cell phone rang. I could not make out what just happened. I did remember how the Lord called Samuel and how the young Prophet knew not the Lord's voice. Shaking that off, I picked it up. This time it was Hustla's number, which was odd for this time of the day for him.

"Hello."

"Hey stranger, how are you?"

"I'm doing good Hustla."

"I didn't think you were going to answer at first."

"I was half sleep but that doesn't matter. How are you all doing?"

"You know she just had our second baby, and you haven't seen the first one yet."

"I will see your children in time."

"When?"

"I don't know."

"Have you even thought about coming back home to help run the funeral home?"

"I haven't really thought about it and if I did, I would just be a thought."

"You know I need you" Hustla said as he spoke with heart.

I was quiet. That was the main reason why I didn't talk to him. He is the only one on this earth who can persuade me against what I think. I heard him speak unsurely, "You there?"

Softly I responded, "I'm here. I wonder if my mom had you calling me because her number came across my screen a little earlier."

"I didn't know she called."

"Yeah, she did."

"That is the other reason you need to come on back."

"Houston."

"Wait you called me Houston" Hustla said with a hint of laughter.

"Yeah, this lets you know I am serious. I left because I didn't like the way she was leading God's people and the secrets, she did behind closed doors. I don't want any part of liars and deceitful people; my mother was both of those."

"She preaches against sin now and has gotten help from drinking."

"Good for her."

"When you left it opened her eyes."

He was quiet for a moment as he spoke, "We miss you. We want you home and not just to help us but to see you."

"I've missed you too but not the lies and deception."

"What about you coming back to help us?"

"What about the life I have here?" I asked.

"I understand you have a life, which, allows you travel time all over the world. It would mean the world to me; to all of us if you would consider coming back. You know I would not ask because I know coming back is a big deal for you. Bobby D. you know I wouldn't ask you if I didn't need you."

This must be serious for him to come out and ask me. I questioned him, "What is it that you really need me for if I come back?"

"Mostly be the undertaker at the funeral home and occasionally pick up bodies. I'll still be the director and arranging funerals, Inga is still the secretary, and your dad writes the policies and gets out in the field doing advertisement."

"What makes you think I will go back in the family business? I may not have renewed my licensure."

"If I know you. I know you would not let it be a waste. Mostly I been praying you could loan us a little of your time and I know you will help me if you can."

He was right. I would help because of him. I asked, "Other than needing me, what else does the business lack?"

"The family car needs of dire repairs. Last week we had a funeral and the car quit. Luckily, we got it back running but the financial state is weak and repairs are almost impossible."

34

"What about the funeral
transportation? How are they all holding up?"

"We got the hearse wagon out the shop
and haven't road tested it yet. Your said he would
check it out."

"You know my dad knows nothing about
cars?" I spoke with laughter.

"I know but I don't think he does. He still
thinks he can fix up to date cars."

"He should stick with the old truck."

I thought for a few more seconds before
saying, "Because you are the closest thing of a
brother I will ever have, and because you have
asked of me, I will come back because of you."

"Yes! You don't know how happy you have
made me" Hustla stated.

"I was headed to Thule."

"Thule?"

"Yes. I wanted to see what it looked like this
time of year."

"Ok, but Thule?" he said slowly.

"Doing things on my bucket list and that was
one of them. Actually, I was going until you
called."

"You see how on time God is. HE knew you
were leaving and had me calling you."

"That and my plane got delayed,
which, forced a hotel for the night."

"Thank you, Jesus" I heard Hustla say.
I was thinking how it is nothing, but God I did not board the plane tonight; as I thought back to the voice I heard before he called. Sounding all happy was Hustla's tone, "I am just glad you are helping. You don't know how much this means me."

"Let me state my conditions first."

"Ok. Name your conditions."

"Don't expect me to actively partake in the church ministry. I am there to embalm the dead, maybe pick them up."

"I won't expect anything less of you but if you see anything that needs improving let me know."
"Next, I'll get a place."

"You can stay with your parents, or you can stay with us."
I was wordless. I hadn't thought about living in my parent's home since I left eight years ago. I questioned him, "Do they know you have asked me for help or to come back?"

"Yes."

"What did they say?"

"They are hoping you come back because they missed you more. They don't care about you living with them. They just want to see you."

"Hustla coming back is not the easiest thing for me. I hope you know and understand that."

"I do and I am grateful you will consider coming back. You have no idea how long I been praying for this."

"If mom talks about why I left and I am not ready to discuss it, I will up and leave like I did all those years ago; this time I will change my number and be another memory."

"I will let them know."

"Ok."

"Bobby D. how much before I get off the phone. Tell me how much will your payments be?"

I was just thinking about that. I know the business use to be ok. I replied, "I am helping. Your money is no good for now. I will work for free until things improve. I would like to see the financial status or quota once a month. Once I see how the business is going then we can discuss payment if I am around long."

"I am thankful for whatever time you offer."

"But I won't take a pay cut just so my mother can have a lavish lifestyle. If that be the case, I won't be paid top dollar. Agreed?"

"Agreed. When can we expect your arrival?"

I thought for a few more seconds because I don't have any more sin jobs. I said, "Maybe the beginning of June. This will give me a little more time in preparing myself psychologically when I see my parents."

"The beginning of June is this coming Sunday" Hustla spoke with surprise.

"I don't know if I will be as prepared, but the military has taught us how to not feel so I might as well get on it."

"Great. I can't wait to see you."

"I know."

"Goodbye, Bobby D."

"Goodbye Hustla."

Hanging up the phone, I laid in bed and reminisced on the few times over the years he and I talked. Whenever he would bring up my mother, I would abruptly end the call. I closed my eyes and wanted some sleep but all I could remember was that day I left without saying goodbye. I guess I had a rude awakening just by seeing her number, and Hustla calling. It is not that I don't have conversations for her, I just don't have a high tolerance for the underhanded characteristics my mother possessed back then.

A few times Hustla told me she has been preaching the truth. I was glad to hear that but I was still not convinced. The Lord has a way of doing things. I hope this is one of HIS doings. With no more work ahead of me, going back doesn't seem like a terrible thing. Oddly enough, I liked making people pay for cheating or lying. This lifestyle has been a blessing. I use earthly talent the military has given me and I tell people what the Word of God says about them doing what they do. Along with my payments from the Elite Sniper Unit, living this way, without knowing or seeing clients has made me a lot of money in offshore accounts.

I don't need anything else for the rest of my life. I am very wealthy, almost thirty, no children, relationship or ties. I come and go as I please, but I know there is something more for me. I can feel it and getting out of physical punishment might be what I need. On the other hand, being an undertaker is my passion. Its' something when you take care of the dead. It fascinates me for some reason how the blood drains out and formaldehyde is pumped to give the body a lifelike appearance. I guess growing up with the dead, preaching to the dead and seeing people alive but dead to the things around them, made me love the dead.

You never fully get it until you see them embalmed before you. It is something about taking pride in preparing a body. Truthfully, I think of it as an artwork that lets you know how valuable life is when you have seen and touched a cold, dead and motionless corpse. I closed my eyes, turned over feeling better about tomorrow.

Chapter 3
June

I arrived back at the airport to exchange my ticket for a ticket home. The entire trip was dreaded. When I touched down at the airport, I felt like a country person in the city for the first time. This airport has played a major part of my life but today it seems strange. It is a Sunday and I, that means church. For the last eight years, I prayed and fasted about this day. But going back home has never been the option for me. If Hustla hadn't called, I might be in Thule by now laying low and no doubt freezing but at peace with myself and all the decisions I have made.

Either which way, I heard the words *nine months; a work to do* and then Hustla calls me. I don't believe in coincidence because there is no such thing. I do still believe in God. I caught a taxi and decided to check in on them unannounced. I know they will be flabbergasted about seeing me, but I want it unscripted. We arrived at my mother's church. I paid the taxi driver, got out and he drove off. I just stood there staring at the huge brick building. I didn't think it would be as hard as it would be, but it was.

An ill sensation came over me, but I shook it off. Upon opening the doors my mother had just turned her back. I eased in and took a seat in the back row. Everything looked the same except many new members. However, I did recognize Mother Clarke with her wide hat on as usual. I searched the place for my father. I didn't see him at first but when I did I wanted to give him a hug. He didn't see me because he was busy being on the front row and paying close attention to my mother as always. Other than that, the place looked brighter and more crowded.

My mother faced the congregation. I could see the years have been kind to her. Then again, she does dye her hair often and looks the same. She spoke with assurance, "You must be thankful for who you are and how things have happened in your life. We as humans get so caught up in what we don't have we forget to be thankful for what we do have. We for some reason unknown believe in our little mind, if we don't have something; something is wrong but it is not."

Everyone was quiet as mother asked, "Are there any announcements?"

Inga stood up to say, "Not at this time, Pastor."

She sat back down as my mother went back to the podium and said with a smile, "Minister Houston, dismiss the congregation."

My mother went to the back like she normally does while Hustla walked to the podium. Soon as he faced the people, he saw me and lifted his hands in a praise to God. No one knew what that was all about, but I did. Inga looked back and saw me. She wanted to shout but I shook my head no very quickly. Hustla was happy and smiling when he gave me that familiar nod. With joy he said, "As I dismiss you all today, you all should know the Lord answers prayers. It may take a time, but God is always on time. I am so thankful everyday but today I am overwhelmed with joy. Let us all stand for dismissal."

Everyone stood up and Hustla said, "With uplifting hands, repeat after me: "Let the words of my mouth and the meditation of my heart be accepted in thy sight. Oh Lord, my strength, my redeemer. Amen."

They all repeated after him as he stated, "Hug someone you hadn't hug before."
I was out the door so fast Hustla barely caught me. when he did I heard, "So, you leaving as fast as you came?"

"No. I didn't want anyone touching me or questioning me."

He gave me a big hug as he whispered, "I'm so glad you are here."

"Only for you."

He let me go as he said, "Let me look at you. All grown up now. I barely knew who you were."

"You look the same. Why didn't you tell me you were preaching now?"

"I didn't want you feeling like you had an obligation because I am Ministering."

"That would not have persuaded me at all and you of all people should know that."

"I did but I didn't want to spring that in on you."

"Now out of respect I will call you Minister Reed or Minister Houston, what?"

"Whatever you decide I am still your cousin Hustla and glad to see you. Has your mother seen you?"

"No."

"I won't force you but come with me before the people start coming out the doors."

He and I walked around the side and it was still the same as he asked, "You like the way things look?"

"It's different but in some ways, it is still the same. The ending message threw me off."

"I told you she been preaching the truth lately."

"That's good."

We arrived at the side entrance of the study. I have used this getaway door many a times in my day. When he opened the door, my parents were in the study alone. My father saw me first as he spoke, "Bobby is that you? Really you?"

"Yes, Sir. It's me, your only child."

He ran and gave me a hug. My dad has always been good towards me and leaving him was the hardest part, but I think was for the best. He looked me over and stated, "You've turned out to be a fine individual and I am so glad you are home. You don't know how many times I had played this day in my head. You have made this old man happy."

"It is good to see you dad. I missed you so much over the years and it pained me to leave without telling you where I was or what I had planned."

My mother came over and said, "My child you look well. May I have a hug also?"

Houston nodded and like a child of long ago, I obeyed my role model. Lifting my arms to hug her, she whispered, "I am glad you back."

She released me and asked, "Where will you be staying? I mean I can't bare it if you don't come back and stay with us."

"I can stay with you all while I am here."

"Surely you are not leaving so soon. You just got here and we haven't had time to catch up or talk. How long you plan on staying?"

"I don't know."

Minister Houston stepped in on my behalf by replying, "Bobby D. is here because I asked. We need help running the funeral home and I know Bobby D. knows the job frontwards and backwards. I would love it if my cousin stayed but however long it takes; that's how long your child, will be here."

"Well put Minister Houston."

"Hustla is the associate pastor here. I mean Houston" my mother mentioned.

I faced him with joy as I responded, "Is there anything else hidden or things you've forgotten?"

"No, but I can't wait for you to meet your nephews."

Mother said, "I am so glad you back with us again. Now my family will do even better."

My dad said, "Come on Gloria you've preached hard today. Let me take you out for supper."

"Would you like to come with us Bobby?"

"No. I'm going over to the funeral home and check things out."

"Today is Sunday" my dad said.

"I know."

They all were quiet as Minister Houston said, "Bobby D. will be fine. We can eat later. I will show everything so Bobby D. will know what is going on."

My parents both gave me a hug as they left out. I said, "Thank you."

Houston faced me again but this time, he stated, "I saw your squirming and gave you a rescue. Besides you just got here, and I don't need you leaving like you did all those years ago."

"I did leave kind of suddenly, didn't I?"

"When I got up and your mom called our house looking for you. She was out of her mind worrying about you. The letter you had sent a few days later was nice but you should have said goodbye in person. I was worried sick about you."

"If I told you in person, you would have made me stay like you always do."

"I only want what is best for you."

"I know but what did the church family say?"

"You know your mother. She told them you left for the military earlier and on some type of top mission."

"Sounds good; almost like the truth."

"Come on you have to meet Inga and the boys first."

"You never told me their names. You only said the boys."

Minister Houston started laughing as he said, "You right, and I just assumed you already knew."

"The five-year old name is Baker and the baby's name is Jr."

"Ok. I am so happy for you."

A knock was heard as Minister Houston said, "Come in."

In walked Inga. Baker ran to Houston, and his dad picked him up. My cousin seems happy about fatherhood. The way they were interacting made me somewhat sorrowful because I didn't have that interaction; neither did Houston. Inga came over and said, "When I saw you, I wanted to scream."

"I know that's why I shook my head no."

"I am happy you here Bobby D. Moreover, I am glad you are helping us."

"Thanks to your husband, no doubt."

She smiled and said, "Houston always allows the Lord to use him. But seriously, you really look amazing. I almost not recognize who you were."

"Glad you didn't know who I was in front of all those nosey people. Cut the mushy stuff out and let me see the baby in your arms."

Inga leaned over and handed me Jr. I leaned in closer and observed how he favors my dad, his uncle. Before I could mention it, my best cousin said, "I already know."

I looked up at him and responded with a kind smile. Inga talked with her husband as I held the baby in my arms. It was funny seeing how small and precious life is at that age; to later watch it grow into all kinds of adjectives and some being bad. It never occurred how holding a frail innocent child, how our lives are innocent, but the environment makes and or shapes us. Some are born with luxury and many into poverty or near poverty level. I was born blessed and fortunate to have hustling parents.

When the married couple finished, I handed Inga the lad. She asked, "You are staying with us because we want you at our house?"

"No. I am staying at my parents."

"Well, that is even better. I hope everything works out for you and us all. Frankly, I am so glad you are here."

Inga gave me another hug as she took the children out with her. Houston stated, "I believe the entire church crowd is gone so we can leave."

I followed him as he locked up. So far coming back hasn't been as challenging as I once thought but a challenge all the same. Minister Houston asked, "How are you traveling?"

"On feet for today but tomorrow, I plan to get some wheels."

"Ok. Anything in mind?"

"Yes, and you will be amazed."

"Bobby D. you always amaze me, and this won't be any different."

I smiled as he and I walked towards his car.

I felt optimistic all of a sudden about being back in this small town. We rode past my parent's home and made our way to the funeral home. It had an odd appeal; which, prompt me ask, "I see you must be in charge of up keeping the grounds?"

Houston laughed as he said, "A little something like that."

"You guys do need my help, and it looks like from the outside in."

"We do. I did tell you we need you."

"What happen to Old man Charley?"

"He passed on and since his passing, I been cutting the yard and doing my best."

"No, offense Houston. I mean Minister Houston."

"Houston is fine."

"Houston no offense but retry your best again."

We both laughed as I spoke more, "I will get someone in here tomorrow on contract to have the grounds kept twice a month in the summer and however often in the winter."

"Thank you."

"Glad I am able."

We pulled into the back like always beside the broken-down hearse with the hood up. I questioned, "I thought you said it was fixed?"

"Something must still be wrong with it. I know your dad was out here yesterday and it must not have crank for him."

"Oh."

I took out the note pad and wrote new vehicles. Houston looked over at me and said, "I see you still take notes."

I made a joke when I stated, "I must especially when dealing with family. You guys are the main ones who forgets how you were helped."

"I think ours is a little better than that."

"If you say so" I said as I put my note pad in my pocket.

Houston laughed as he got out. As I stood under the huge car porch I stared at the Cremation building. Many times, I have cremated people, and each one is done differently; therefore, it never gets old.

"Are you coming in?" Houston yelled at me as he unlocked the back door. I walked up as he opened the door, and he turned on the light. The familiar smell rushed my nose. I inhaled as long as I could before exhaling, slowly. We walked down the eight feet wide hall. The place still had the same look about it on the inside but brighter. We walked past the refrigeration room, and I felt a rush like no other. I stopped and opened the door as Houston said, "I see you still remember your favorite place in the whole building."

"How could you ever forget the very first time you touched a lifeless body. It's something about the way you have the power."

"Ok. You are scaring me now" Houston spoke with laughter.
I smiled as I walked further inside the room. The area was still the same but not as cold. I asked, "Why is the room not cold? You know the temperature must be freezing. If not, the bodies could thaw."

"Bobby D. do you see any bodies in here?"

"No, but when they do come, you don't want them at room temp either."

"Ok. I will turn up the temp" Houston said as he walked towards the thermostat. The AC kicked in. He turned around and asked, "Is that better?"

"It is once I see if the room still gets cold."

"We haven't had a problem in here so hopefully this should be fine."

"When is the last time a body been in here?"

"It has been about three weeks."

"Who you had before then?"

"We had a part time undertaker, but he found a full-time job on the other side of town and we need you until we can get someone."

I only shook my head as I continued to stare all around. He asked, "You finished looking in here?"

"Yeah. We can stop back by on our way out. That should give the room cool time."

Houston walked out first as I closed the airtight door. We walked before stopping at the embalming room. The light came on. I was back in love with my first love. The table where the bodies are prepared was spotless. The air reaped of death and decomposition. I smiled as I walked slower towards the cabinets. I opened them up for inventory and almost everything was gone. I questioned, "When the last person left, what all did they take?"

"Nothing I guess."

"Looks like you all need some of everything."

"What we need can be put on a list for Inga. She makes orders every Monday."

I took out my note pad and wrote down all the materials needed. I put it back in my pocket. Houston kept watching me because he never liked this part of the mortuary business and I didn't care for the public eye. It has never been easy to console a grieving family when they have lost a loved one. Sometimes you don't know what to say and sometimes words can't express the pain one goes through. Houston snapped fingers and asked, "You about finished in here?"

"Almost. I think that person ripped you all off."

"There is no way you should be this low on all these items."

"He probably didn't order enough when he sent in the inventory list."

"Maybe but still. These items should always be in full stock. You never know when you have more than one body at a time."

"That is why I am glad you are here. You are a precise organizer."

Ignoring him, I picked up and needles and stated, "You see this needle."

Houston walked over and said, "What about it?"

"It is worn and has been broken. I bet when the guy was doing injections it broke. The body was perhaps frozen and wasn't properly massaged to loosen up the tendons or muscles."

"Throw away all you see fit Bobby D."
I threw them away and took out my not pad to add them to the list. I asked, "How financial stable is the company?"

Houston blew out a sigh as he said, "It's steady but not as it could be. We all have taken pay cuts to keep the place afloat. You can check them out later."

I made my way over and said, "I take it you all still let my mother spend and spend."
He didn't say a word as I stated, "If you all want my financial help, you will not allow her any spending money that is not there. Inga can't keep fixing the books because this place will get audited and someone will be in jail as the business goes under. Exactly how much in debt is this place?"

"I don't think your mom is the problem, but the place is about twenty thousand."

"Twenty thousand?"

"Yeah, and that is pushing it."

"How did it get that way? Mom has the money from the church. She doesn't have any ties in the business so how does she get her hands on it?"

"If anything, it is from your dad. She doesn't ask me or Inga. I don't think she touches the money at all, but I don't know."

"Either you tell him, or I will. I will not put my money in this place to help save something my mother will only take down the drain as soon as I leave. Someone should tell her about it; unless you have twenty thousand for her."

"Bobby D. you are right but that's if she has her hands on it."

"Houston, she has always been like that, but do you know why I left?"

He was quiet. I waited for him to say something. Houston my only friend said, "I have often wondered why you left. When I found out you were last in the office with your mom, I knew she had a part in it."

"Houston, she was the main reason why I left. I got tired of the way she was misusing the people of God, drinking and cursing as if it were ok. On the real, it made me sick every time she would say one thing and do another. I watched her and I didn't like the vision, so I changed the scenery. She has made me turn my back on God and HIS s- called calling. I told her if God called me to do as she does, HE could keep HIS calling. I didn't want any part of it."

"I see now when you left, she said, she was sorry that you both didn't end right."

"I didn't want anything to do with church or God. In fact, when people disobeyed God, I sought after them for real people of God."

"Bobby D. you can't justify one wrong with another. If the people you worked for, sought some type of vengeance for people or whatever then they too are just as guilty."

"I always knew that, but I didn't want to accept it until now."

"However way you do things, we are not to partake in another man's sins. Have you done true repentance?"

"Honestly. I know what I did was morally wrong, but I don't feel sorry for it. I can't repent for something I believe was rightly justified."

"That is all up on you but when you want to talk about it I am here for you as always."

"Thank you, Houston but we have some more of this place to see" I spoke to get his mind off me and my old outside job.

Chapter 4

We left out the door. Next, we walked across the hall to the personal care room. It is here the makeup artist bathes the body and does the makeup. I don't know what all they need so I asked, "Who is the artist in here?"

"We have a lady that comes in and does it for us."

"Is she full time of part time?"

"She is part time whenever we can get her, but you can do it if you want."

"Ok."

We left out and went to the casket room. Those caskets were still brand new and in shape. I smiled as I remembered how Houston and I scared a couple that was picking out caskets. Houston walking them around and showing them the ones they wanted. When they got to the one I was in, he lifted the lid, and I said Boo. The woman hollered and took out running. I laughed but my dad didn't think it was funny. I was only fifteen and at that time in my life; this was all I really knew.

Houston and I went up the hall a few feet. Here are the four grieving rooms, which are located across from each other with closing doors. I only stuck my head in. They appeared neat, in order and unused in a while. I closed each door as he opened the hall door. On each side of the hall door are restrooms and a large sitting room. On the left of the large sitting room; with the secretary office door to the right, my dad's office and Houston's offices are further to the left with the entrance doors straight ahead. But down the hall is a small room that has a twin bed. I would use if it got late or if I was tired to drive.

I would sleep in that room and that room became my second home away from home. Houston asked, "Well what do you think?"

He broke my thoughts. I replied in a slow tone, "I think this place can be turned around if you keep my mother out its pocket."

"I will talk with her and make sure she is not touching these funds."

"If you want my help, you better do more than talk. You better keep her itchy hands off this funeral business money and keep it on the church's money."

Houston didn't say a word. He knows I will tell her and will not care for throwing her hissy fit. He smiled as I said, "Let's go and check back on the refrigeration room on our way out."

I walked down the hall back and opened the door. The room was freezing cold and just the way it should be. He faced me as he asked, "Is that better?"

"Houston, keep it this way" I stated with a smile.

Houston turned the light off as he closed and locked the door back door. I got in the car as Houston got in. With no more putting it off, I spoke, "Take me to my parent's home. I am tired and need the rest."

We drove about two miles, and he pulled in the driveway. I sat there for a minute because I remember my childhood as if it were happening all over again. I could have walked but I know Houston would not have it, besides he stays about five blocks over. Me sitting in his car in their driveway must have been long because he asked quietly, "You go to be ok?"

"Yeah. I was born here."

"I know. We both were raised here."

"I know" I said with a smile.

"Bobby D. for what it is worth, I am glad you are here. I really am."

"I came because this is one of my fears."

"If you need me; you know where I am."

I got out and closed the door. Houston left out as I walked towards the house. My parents were still gone. The front door wasn't locked. I thought they would have changed by now, but I guess not. I walked into the living room and the only thing changed was the furniture. *Mother's taste is more expensive* I thought. On the walls and on the

59

stands, were pictures of Houston and I. Parts of me thought she would have taken pictures of me down, but she hadn't?

Making my way towards the open room under the stairs, I turned the light on and laid on the couch. I have slept more in this room with the small full bath than I did in my own queen size bed upstairs. It was always something about this room that makes me feel comfortable. Many nights I would get out of my own bed and sleep on this couch. Every morning my dad would find me here and wouldn't say a word. *Oh, how I miss those days of long ago,* I thought as I got up and put my one bag on the chair, turn the light off and lay back down on the couch.

The darkness was scary black. No sound was heard but the silent whip of the ceiling fan in this room. I could see what looks like flashing red lights. My heart raced by itself. The more I closed my eyes the brighter the red lights appeared. I jumped up and the lights disappeared. Swallowing hard, I turned on the light and went in the kitchen for a drink of water. Closing my eyes, I sighed and turned the lights back off and laid back down.

I just laid there not knowing and understanding what the flashing red lights. I turned my head and drifted off to sleep. This time I felt a cold hand on me. I jerked up and there was nothing there. *I know I am not crazy or losing it* I thought as I laid flat on my back on the couch. I wanted sleep but it didn't want me. I didn't feel like reading and I didn't feel like praying. It's just ironic how I grew up in a home that demonstrated Jesus is the answer but after seeing the way my mother misused the people and their funds; I shun my face before the Lord. I don't understand how HE could let my mother go on so long and not punish her?

Every day since my youth, I always heard how the calling of God on your life is something you should embrace but the way the calling looks to me, I still don't want it. I turned over on my side and stated in a whisper, *"Lord what you want with me? I have served you or calling myself serving you in my youth until I saw how a calling can be. To be here is what I don't want but they need my help. I feel myself turning and pushing further and further back like I did all those years ago. I don't mean to be out of your Will but I don't know. What I do know is that my mother has caused me to stumble. She has made me not believe anymore and there is nothing more to say. Amen."*

Without my knowledge, I fell asleep and, in this sleep, I kept hearing, *you have a work to do, you have a work to do.* I jumped up in a cold sweat. I glanced at the clock, and it read eight AM. I was surprised I slept all night and didn't hear my parents when they came in. I got up and took a short bath before they could awake. I was on my way out the door when I heard my father say, "Bobby."

I turned around and he was standing there like he had done many times in my past.

"Yes dad?"

"You want some breakfast?"

"No. I can get something while I am out."

"Your mother is still sleep. Would you like some company?" he asked in a way that was not possible to leave him behind.

I know he wants to rebuild his relationship with me but there was never anything too wrong with his relationship with me. I smiled and said, "If you want to tag along, I don't see why not."

He got put his wallet in his pocket and headed out the door behind me as he asked, "You need me to bring the truck, or do you want to walk like always?"

I didn't think of transportation. I am so used to walking all over this town that I didn't think of the many stares and questions I would encounter for being gone too long. I replied, "You can bring your truck."

"You want to drive?"

"No, dad. You drive and I will tell you where."

"Ok, that'll work for me."

He stepped back in and got his keys. Seconds later he came out and we got in his truck. My dad seemed happier as he asked, "Where too?"

"Let's go look at some better vehicles and a hearse wagon."

Dad turned onto the highway and began driving. One main thing I liked about my dad was unmaterialistic he is. My dad pickup truck has been running since the beginning of time. He keeps it properly serviced and running well. I thought, *this maybe the only thing he can work on that won't give him a problem.* Bothering my thoughts was my dad's confident voice, "She still rides like brand new; doesn't she?"

"She sure does dad" as I replied without looking at him. When I did, I saw how he kept his eyes focused. He spoke, "I know you may not want to talk about why you left but you should know I love you, Bobby D. You are my only child, and I love you today, just as much as I did when you were born."

"Dad you were never the reason for me leaving. You can be a push over sometime but not a problem. It was mom; your wife."

He kept his face straight when he stated, "I know she can be a handful at times, but she is your mother. I have always been a sucker for her and it's like that because I love her."

"Dad you can love someone and tell them right or you can love someone and say nothing. Half the time you would not say a word when you knew she is in error. She misuses church funds and makes the people do what she wants. How is that God because I am not getting it?"

"You right but we all will give into account for our own sins as well as actions; even if some are what we call right."

"I just wish you would have stood up or did something."

"Something like what?"

"I don't know. She tricks everyone with her slick speech. My mom is a master of persuasion. Back then, many of those people were not ready for the Buzzards Hangout. I bet many of them fell by the wayside and she probably got mad."

"Many of them did fall but Bobby but you are looking at it all wrong."

"How is that?"

"She tells them the Word but that is all she can do."

"Same thing she said."

"She was right. It is up to every one of us and them to discover who Jesus is in their life. She can tell us what the Word says but she can't show us because she is just like us; striving to make it in. I must admit, she tells one thing and lives another, but we all have in some form."

Plainly without emotions I told my dad, "She is a preacher. She isn't supposed to curse, drink and lie. She should be an example and after seeing her example, I made up my mind to not walk in a "calling" but to let it bypass me as I live my life."

"It doesn't always work like that my child. You should figure out what is best for you and make your decision on what you think but the Lord Jesus can guide you if you ask of HIM."
He was quiet the rest of the trip because he was telling me the truth. My mother in her sick way, in some form has turned me away from God. I don't like hearing about a calling or any type of prophesy. I once believed but now I believe as it is convenient for me to believe. So far, I am doing just fine with my own belief system. It's not that I don't believe in Christ, I do. I just have my own way of believing.

We arrived at the vehicle car lot for funeral homes. I saw all kinds or makes and models. I know they need a flower van, hearse wagon and a family car. My dad was looking around and suddenly something about the thing caught my eye. It was a dark blue hearse wagon. My dad came over with a question, "You like that huh?"

"I do" I said softly.

"It is brand new and too high for our budget."

"Dad you might be on a budget, but I am not."

The man saw us looking as he approached. I asked, "If I bought this hearse wagon, the matching family car and the flower van. Will you give us a deal?"

"If I can give you a deal I will. The hearse is used and it's the only one I have. For that one, I would say about six thousand dollars. The family car is used but in meant condition and it's nine thousand. The flower van is used and on sale for five thousand."

"Sir. Either you will give us a deal, or you won't? I didn't ask about the year or this and that. All I need to know is if you will give us a deal?"

"I sure will. What kind of deal are you looking at?"

"For all three, cash money right here today; how much?"

"Nineteen thousand."

"Eighteen and you have a deal."

He looked at me and said, "Since it is for the church, I can do that."

"Let's get the paperwork" I said as the man walked off.

My dad asked, "Bobby D. why are you spending money when you can fix the ones we have up?"

"Dad, you been patching on them since I left and you still patching on them. It's ok. I am not asking for the money back. It'll pay for itself." I walked off from my father. I saw him calling on his phone; I just hope he isn't calling my mother. I don't need nor want her hands out because if she extends them, I may cut them off. The man was sitting at his desk drawing up the paperwork. I gave him my ID and the check. He called the bank to make sure it was legit, and it was. He asked, "What funeral home will all this be going?"

"The Final Resting Place."

With such surprise he yelled out, "Oh! Over there where that lady pastor preaches?"

"She preaches at the church down the street from there but yes."

"Oh ok. My daughter got saved under her and now preaches at her own church up north in Indiana. Can't wait to tell my daughter I met Pastor's Reed's family."

"That's nice. Is the paperwork about finished?" I stated to change the subject.

"Yes. You will get the original title for the vehicles once you file at the courthouse. Thank you so much for doing business with us."

We stood up and I stated, "Someone will be back for the other vehicles today, if not in the morning."

"That will be fine. You've bought them and no one will get them."

He handed me my keys. I went out the door with my paperwork. My dad said, "How are we going to get them out here today?"

I handed dad the other two keys because I made my claim, "I am driving the hearse wagon. I bought them, you figure out who can drive them back to the funeral home. I'm putting insurance on all these vehicles."

I didn't hear anything else he was saying. My eyes were solely fixed on the beautiful wagon. The top of it was like a rag top but it was a darker blue than the rest of the car. When I opened the door, I felt happy. I eagerly sat in the driver's seat for I will be the one driving this one. This is my baby, Old Blue. I turned on the ignition. I barely heard the motor. I turned on the air and it was cold and to my liking. Taking my hand, I rubbed the right side of the seat. I closed my eyes for it was soft and wonderful under my hand.

When my eyes opened and my dad was already gone in the family car. I fixed my mirrors and drove off. I took my time and rode around town. Everywhere I stopped people were looking and expecting a coffin in the back. I thought *a coffin in the back, or a roller cot would be a nice touch.* I liked the idea as I filled the gas tank up. I drove off and went to the funeral home. When I got there and parked out back and put my list of items on the front seat so I can give it to Inga.Houston came outside as I parked the car under the car porch.

I got out of the car and walked towards him as he approached the front of the car. He had a Christmas smile on his face as he asked with a humongous smile, "You bought a hearse for the funeral home?"

"No. I bought me a hearse, but the funeral home can use but I will be driving it."

Houston stared at me as if I was lying but he knows I don't do that. He chuckled as he questioned "Bobby D. why didn't you get a regular vehicle?"

"I am not a regular person, and you know that."

"Yeah, but a hearse?"

"Yeah. I'm not doing anything pleasurable here but embalm the dead and help out."

"Don't leave out, getting things right with your mother."

"That is up in the air, not open for discussion and wasn't a part of the plan."

"You right. Take your time."

We were both quiet as I said, "I also bought a family car; which my dad is driving by the way where is he at?"

"I don't know. I thought he was still with you."

"He left out while I was admiring the car."

"You know he still drives slow."

Just as we were speaking my dad drove up with a smile. Houston asked as he got out, "You all smiles today."

"Bobby D. that car rides on air."

We all laughed as I stated, "Who going to go the flower van?"

"I can take Inga" my dad stated as we both just shrugged.

My dad went inside for Inga. Houston smiled while saying, "You bought vehicles?"

"Didn't we need them?"

"We do but I didn't expect you to buy them all at one time. How much do we owe you?"

"Nothing. I donated them but I will drive the hearse for my own use."

Before he could answer, my dad came out with Inga. She said, "I told Deacon Reed I will go in the family car but not in the hearse."

I laughed as my dad responded, "Bobby D. is driving that."

"Bobby D. you can keep that car to yourself."

"You work in a funeral home. You can't be afraid of the dead."

"It's not that, I don't like the idea of being in a hearse alive. I don't care if I am in the front. A hearse is still a hearse."

I laughed at her as she left with my dad. Houston stated, "Let me go back inside I have some arrangements to make. Oh, Bobby D. did you have the order list for Inga?"

"Yeah."

I went back over to the driver side of the car and got the list. I closed the door and handed it to Houston. He looked over the list and stated, "One day I am going to try my hand at embalming only."

"You went graduated from the same hard knock mortuary school I went too. You know how to do it."

"I know but you have a Ph. D. in Mortuary Science, and you can also be a director and write policies. You are licensed to sign off just like I am in case I am out."

"Forget all about that. So, you want to embalm?"

"I really don't once you think about it. You have all types of cadavers to come in and you never know what diseases they have. I will leave all that up on you" Houston spoke with humor.

"You could have done the embalming if I hadn't come back."

"I could have but not as well as you. Bobby D. you have a knack for making the dead look so much alive and you do it so wonderfully. When you get done, you make the body look well enough to get up and walk off. They look like they are sleeping or taking a nap."

"Thank you. I think of it as an art and right now I am ready to do some work."
We laughed as he went back in the building. I got in the hearse wagon and went to my parent's home. When I got there, sleep was all I wanted, or I thought I was sleep. I kept hearing the words, *nine months. I give you nine months. Nine months.* The tone caused me to wake up and look around. I know I have heard that sound before but can't remember. *Why am I thinking about nine months anyway?* I thought. I saw it was indeed July and from July to March is nine months but then what? Deciding to brush it off I went back to sleep.

July
Chapter 5

The next couple of weeks flew by and July is almost way over; with one week left. I've only had the privilege of embalming many people from the nursery home. At this rate, they don't even need me. Houston came in as I was sitting out front. He stood in his door frame proud as he stated, "Bobby D. you know other than a houses and cars, a funeral is one of the largest purchase a person will have to decide on?"

"That is true if we lived in a highly crime rated area with a lot of people killing but right now, I see a lot of houses and cars being bought." Houston fell out laughing. Inga came in with the oldest boy, Baker. He ran to his dad and gave him a hug. I got up and went to the embalming room for inventory check. I sat in my chair and began writing my list. Before I could finish it all, I heard the door close. I turned around and it was Baker. I asked, "What are you doing in here?"

"I was seeing what you were doing."

"You must leave out because children are not allowed back in here alive."

"You can't tell me what to do. My dad runs this place and one day I will too."

"Little boy as of right now, your dad is a worker here like me. Leave out and don't come back if I don't tell you too, ok."

I started back writing as the lad proclaimed like a champ, "My name is Baker Reed and I am not a little boy. I am old enough and you weird."

I froze as I turned around. My entire persona changed as I said above a whisper, "You are right. I can show you what I do back in here; since you are a big boy and all."

Baker walked closer to the table. I got up and I lifted him up onto the table. He asked, "Is this the table you drain the blood?"

"Lay back and let me show you how it is almost done?"

The child lay back on the sterile table. I strapped the child down and the child asked, "Will you hurt me by showing me what you do in here?"

"I won't hurt you, Baker. You are family."

Baker was quiet as I gave him confidence that I would not do him any harm. I smiled when I said, "Lets' you are a normal body without disease or anything. You had a heart attack and died. They bring you to me and when I get the go ahead from the family I put on my protective gear, which includes, gloves, eye goggles, aprons and guard piece for my mouth and nose.

Before I can start, I must make sure you are
not alive. Are you alive?"

"You know I am" he said with a giggle.

I thought silently, *you won't be giggling
when I finish.* I said, "The first thing an undertaker
must do is to verify the body is indeed stiff and
dead. I can't embalm someone who is still alive;
although, there have been cases when the body was
in a dead state but not dead."

"Can you do that to a live person?" Baker
questioned with excitement.

"I can but it won't be pretty."

The little boy was listening earnestly as
I stroll over to him and leaned in closer.
Speaking softly my words were, "Once I make sure
you are dead, I slowly undress you by cutting away
your clothes with huge shears and if you have on
shoes, I take them off slowly; as to not disturb the
body."

I moved to his feet and picked them
up slowly as I took off his shoe one by one. I could
feel him trembling. He was watching my every
movement. *I have his full attention* I thought as I sat
the shoes on the opposite table. Making my way to
him, I stated "Once you are naked as the day you
were born, I check your body for tattoo markings,
bruises, catheters, pacemakers and anything out the

ordinary; all of this is for insurance purposes and to make sure you are who you are."

I picked up a plain bottle and stated with low tone before squirting him with water, "Next I usually grab the spray bottle to spray the face and sometimes the eyes will shoot open and stare right into my face."
He hollered as he yelled out, "I don't want to hear any more!"

Sounding almost angry, I screamed lowly, "Too bad you should have listened when I said get out. Since you are old enough as you told me earlier, you will now finish participating."
I waited for the little boy to protest but he just laid there in a fright. I spoke closer to his face, "I must clean the face for a decaying body will start in this area as it breaks down. It's like if you haven't eaten all day your breath will stink; that stink is the smell of flesh dying but picture if you will, an entire body smelling like a big bad breath."
When I said that, I put the spray bottle down and grabbed the little boy's tied leg with one hand and pretended washing it. Baker began crying some for his mom. I called out, "Dead bodies can't talk with their mouths. Their body tells the story so shut up and let me get your story, Baker."

"I don't want you to get my story. Please let me go."

My ears did not hear him as I stated, "Once the body is cleaned with soap and water, I go for my tools."

I walked over to the opposite counter and picked up my tools. Baker was whining as I stated, "Don't cry. There is so much more you must learn of the family business."

Baker had a tear come out of his eye. I wiped it away and stated, "I must make incisions to drain blood and fluids from the head, the rest of the body with a trocar, and suction the fluids from the organs with the aspirator."

I went to the desk and picked up the hollow tube trocar instrument. I went back over to Baker and showed him the long, thick needle looking tool. He started pouting and moving. Smiling from the inside, I spoke quietly, "Shush Baker, I am merely showing you what I do, since you will run this business one day like your daddy."

He shook his head back and forth as I continued, "This tube is sharp like a needle and empty like one. You can drain the blood first of suction the organs first. I mostly drain the blood but today I will suction your organs first. The first place I put it is right above your navel."

I lifted his shirt and fear was everywhere. I made the tool touch his body. He jumped from the contact. I stated, "I won't hurt you. Why do you think hunters gut the stomach first? Let me tell you why. It is because the stomach is where the most gases develop and give major problems. This is the same with humans. We have dangerous gases in us and when we die, they can cause more harm to the undertaker, like myself. Embalming them can be difficult when one is designing a body for perfection. If I don't embalm you, your funeral must be within a day or so and with a closed casket."

Baker tried to remain calm, but it was hard. I continued by saying, "Once this aspirator is inside you, I'll move the tool slowly back and forth for the suctioning fluids off your organs. This tool will even suck up any urine, filthy bowels and gases from your stomach as it goes down the drain. Then I do the heart and lungs the same way with another cut. Think of it like a vacuum sucking up dirt off a dirty floor. This works the same way by pulling water, food and fluid from you. When I am finish, I will add cotton to other holes and put a trocar plug for sowing you up later. Baker fear not. God is not the author of fear but of peace, love and a sound mind. When you leave out of here, I promise you will be a changed little boy."

I unhook the trocar and aspirator. Carefully, I watched him, and he just laid there not knowing if he should move or not. I put the instruments on the table and brought back a knife as I said, "I must cut

78

that big vein in your neck and insert another tool to drain your blood in the special system."

I touched his neck, and he said, "Your hands are too cold."

"I work among the dead they have to be cold."

We stared at each other for a moment as I spoke on, "When your blood leaves your body, I massage your legs for any remaining blood to drain through the tube. I can't leave a drop of blood or at least I try not to. That is why I take my time when I perform this skill. However, I do the head last with an arterial tube. Once all your blood is gone, I can use a chemical called sodium citrate. This will keep the vessel walls open for the embalming fluid can flow easily. Today I will start with the face first."

Baker was watching me as he shook and shook no. I stated, "If the face is full, I won't use cotton behind the eye lids so the eyes won't look like they are sinking. Since your face looks fine, I won't glue them shut. Next, I work on the mouth." From the looks of it, I am scaring him and that is my intention. He will learn to listen until then, he is being taught a valuable lesson. I pretended to examine his body for the perfect vein when I said, "Your jaw looks perfect. I don't need to add cotton to form your mouth or jaw line. You can either glue the mouth shut or you can do what I like to do."

"What do you like to do?" he asked.

"I like to put a big needle in the mouth and sow the gums together before gluing the mouth shut. When I finish, I put cream on your face so the skin on your face won't dry out. I sow you up from the cutting so when the fluid starts, I can see if you are leaking and fix it or perhaps put you on a pair of plastic underwear. Being that you are a boy, I can only pack your butt with cotton. If you were a girl, I would pack your butt and your private with cotton. I am only showing you how I drain blood.
You must hold still. If you close your eyes and pray to God, you might not feel a thing."

I went over to the famous embalming machine and held up the plastic tube as I stated, "I would turn it on and show you how it pumps girly pink fluid that takes the place of cold red blood after I have cut your jugular vein but I don't think you are ready for that, are you Baker?"

The facial expression he gave me was priceless as he cried out, "Please let me go. I won't be a bad boy again."

"Do you really promise not to be bad; since we can't make promises we can't keep?"

"I vow. I won't be bad."

He said vow. Not too many kids would use those words because they would normally say promise. I was prompt to ask, "Do you believe in God? I don't mean because your dad is a preacher but do you really with all your heart, believe in God?"

With no hesitation, Baker announced, "I do believe in God. I do believe in the almighty power of Jesus Christ."

I showed the child the instrument and he whined and pouted in a small prayer. I stated, "You are willing to die alive for your faith?"

"I will die for my faith but don't want to die because I ain't been filled with God's Spirit yet."

"You sure you want God's Spirit? I've seen how people act with it and they didn't act godly at all. Tell me, are you Baker really sure you want God's Spirit ruling and reigning in your body?"

"Yes, I am sure" he spoke as he closed his eyes in a calm state.

I waited for to see if he would talk again. Baker opened his eyes. Out of the purest heart of a child, I heard, "Let me down, please. I won't talk too much ever again."

"You are begging after you on your own wanted to see what it is I do, after I told you to leave out or are you begging in hope I would stop?"

"I won't come back in here as Jesus is my God."

Baker's complexion had become brighter as he mentioned his faith. I know his dad is teaching him the correct way and it means a lot to see this child of great faith. I asked, "Do you think God can stop me from embalming you?"

"I do believe my God Jesus has my life in HIS hands and if it is HIS Will there is nothing neither one of us can do about it."

I gave him a cold stare before smiling. I was pleased with his answers. I spoke with ease, "Because you believe in Jesus with all your heart, I will let you go with one condition."

"What is it?" he asked weakly.

"You serve Jesus with all your heart and do not let anyone make you lie, steal or cheat in any way or do things that would stop you from being HIS servant. Do we have a deal?"

"We have a deal."

I unstrapped the minor and put him down. He was shaking and nervous as I said, "The next time, you won't be so lucky."

The child took out running. I sat down in my chair and thought about what I almost did. I remembered how I once had great faith until my mother kept pushing me. Back then I could have done great work but now I don't' even mention a calling or doing a work. The thought of having a live cadaver was turning me on. I got up and began cleaning off the table again.

Houston was in his office as I stopped by and said, "Baker was in the embalming room. I'm sure he won't come back."

Houston laughed while speaking, "Did you scare him like I did you all those years ago?"

"No, I didn't pretend to be dead. I put him on the table and told him the steps in how I drain blood."

Houston laughed as he said, "He better not have nightmares. If he does, I am coming to see you."

"Come on. He should have left out when I told him."

"That boy of mine acts like his mom sometimes; with his free spirit."

"Where is Inga at anyway?"

"She is running a few last-minute errands for the funeral on Saturday."

"The body is in the casket and ready for the family viewing on tomorrow."

"What time is it, Houston?"

"It's not even ten o'clock."

"It is early."

"Bobby D. you don't know how glad I am about you are helping us."

"Yeah, yeah, yeah."

We laughed as I spoke, "I have a special list for Inga. Give it to her."

"Where you off too?" he asked as he took the list from me.

"The grocery store for snacks."

"If you don't mind stop by Mother Clark."

"And do what?" I said in an ugly tone.

"She wrote it out but didn't sign it."

"Ok, but you know that old bat is my mother's ace."

"She also has the money so the rest of us can get paid."

"I guess so since you put it that way. I'll stop by."

He handed me the check in an envelope. I went out the door and got in my hearse. I didn't want to go to her house because let alone talk to her; especially if I'm not talking to my own mother. I drove slowly to her house. I saw it and smiled devilishly while backing up in her driveway. I bumped the horn and she didn't come out. I got out with the check and walked towards the front door. People were standing around and not moving. I know they wonder if I am here for a body. Getting out, I saw old people staring; therefore, I waved while walking to the front door.

A strong voice called out, "Who is it?"

"It's Bobby D. Mother Clark."

She cracked the door a little. When she saw it was really me she opened it wider asking, "Your mom sent you here?"

"No, ma'am. Houston sent me because you didn't sign your check. I don't remember which one it was, and I didn't look at the check before it was sealed."

"Oh. Come on in and have a seat."
I went inside, and it looked like I was back in time. She had all kinds of old pictures of her and the late Martin Luther King, Jr. and Reverend Jessie Jackson. She had few pictures of her daughter and grandchildren. I looked around and said, "I don't need to sit. I just come for you to sign it so I can go."

I handed her the envelope as she questioned, "What's your rush? You don't have anything to do but work around dead people."

"The dead is better than the live."

She glanced at me and replied with a small attitude, "Let me get my glasses."
She went in her kitchen and came back. I was still standing as she said, "Didn't I tell ya to have a seat? You're not growing anymore."

Giving her a short smile, I sat down. She took the check from me and asked, "I thought I signed it?"

She stared at it longer and spoke, "This doesn't look like my writing. I swear every other month that gal Inga would lose her head if it wasn't attached. Every time I look around, she is losing a check or stating I didn't sign it. I may be old, but I know they are stealing. They have to be. I spend good money every week at the church and yet, they act like the church, and the funeral home is broke. I don't believe it."

"I don't know about any of those things. I was only asked to come by on my way to the grocery store."

"What are you going in there for?"

"I wanted some snacks. Any more questions, ma'am?"

"Since you opened the door, why haven't ya talked to ya mom? You ain't got but one mother and you act like you can get another one like that. You didn't call her or come see her all the eight years you were gone. Was you scared of something, or you want your own sex and knows at Reed Chapel U. L. M. it is highly preached against."

Mother Clark was really working on my nerves with her nosey questioning. Politely I replied, "That is none of your concern why my mother and I haven't talked."

Before she could respond, a knock was heard on the door. She went to the door and asked, "Who is it?"

"It's me Amanda."

Mother Clark peeped through the door before opening it. Standing in the door was an older woman with shiny white hair on a medium frame. It must be her neighbor as the lady stated, "I was just checking on you, Mary."

They laughed as Mother Clark said, "Pastor Reed's child came over to bring me a check to sign. You know I have to look over it and make sure it is all up to par."

"How you do Ma'am? I'm Bobby D."

"I'm Mrs. Amanda Miles. I just joined the burial over there as well as the church. Your mother is an awesome leader, and I enjoy her Words from God every Sunday now."

"That's good Ma'am."

She looked back at Mother Clark and said, "Mary. I didn't know what was going on. Back in my day, to see a hearse wagon in your yard was a sign of bad luck."

"Amanda, I am blessed and don't need luck here."

"I had to make sure. It is kind of odd for someone in a hearse with no body."

They laughed as Mother Clark said, "As strange as it is, a body will be back there shortly. Bobby Reed may have come for me."

"Oh, cut that out, Mary. You, silly girl. You are as healthy as a horse or two."

"Sometimes this old heart of mine reminds me how I am getting old and weary."

"You every bit of twenty-eight" her friend stated.

"Reverse it and you know how I really feel" Mother Clark stated with a smile.

They laughed and I stood there indulging their pointless chattering. The rest of their conversation went on deaf ears as I sighed and spoke, "Excuse me. I don't mean to interrupt but I need you to sign it so I can get back."

"I didn't mean to pry. Let me let you handle your business, Mary."

"It was no trouble. I am glad you came by and checked on me."

"I was coming later but when that car pulled up, I decided I better come on."

"Take care Amanda, love you ole friend."

They hug as the visiting lady said, "Bye now, Mary. Love you my dear friend. Bye."

"Bye" Mother Clark said broke the embrace and closed the door.

She faced me and said sternly, "Now back to answering you. Anything that upsets the pastor is my concern. She can't pray for us if she is having a conflict with her only child"

She stopped talking as she looked me up and down to finish saying, "Who disappears then comes back just as strange as they left."

I was being nice when I responded, "If you don't want to sign it, give it back so I can leave because I refuse to discuss my personal business with you or my mother."

"I ain't ready for you to leave and if I don't want to give it back I won't. It's my check."

She got in my face and continuing saying, "You have any idea the type of crap you took my dearly pastor through? She was at her wits end preaching and worrying about you. She started drinking and having behavior was unlike her. I vowed if I saw you again before these eyes closed was letting you know that you will not do that again. I helped built the church long before you were even thought about and I won't let you destroy my leader with your "*I don't want a calling on my life attitude*. Get with the program and stop hurting my leader."

I could tell her my mother was doing all of that before I left but that too is none of her business. As nicely as I could without freaking out I stated with a sincere warning, "Mother Clark, please remove yourself from my personal space because the answers you seek are none of your affair."

"I am the elder and you are a mere child. You can't tell me what to do especially in my own house."

I stepped back from her and she walked up on me again. I was angry as I stated, "Mother Clark please leave me alone and let me leave.
You talking about things you don't know about. It's evident you don't know a whole lot about your lovely pastor."

"I know you left here odd to always be by yourself and you came back eerie to still be by yourself but having money."

"I'm odd and eerie because I don't spit lies like my mother to people believing in her?"
Mother Clark gave me a few feet as she checked me out up and down as if she were a teenage drama queen to say, "You never dated and probably a virgin even if you are a nice looking."

"Mother Clark I don't mean to cut you off but please back all the way up and let me out your house. I have phobia when someone is too close and you're doing just that."
She continued standing in my way. This time as she taunted me with words her face was nearly my face, "You need a whipping. Your parents were always too busy to give it to you and you come back here and you don't even talk to your mother. You seldom at services and you stay out of everyone's

sight. You only show up at funerals. If that's not peculiar, then I don't know what is."

I tried easing my way around her and she stepped in my way to provoke me. I stated, "Mother Clark you don't know anything about me or the training I have. I would advise you to back up and let me out this house at once. I will not ask again."

"I'm not letting you out until you talk about your mother."

"Please don't make me hurt you" I said again to warn her.

"You can't hurt anything because I am just as swift as you. Your mother always said you were strange and unusual. I believe she is right. May God bless your damned soul Bobby D."
Doing my best to remain calm I asked her again nicer, "Mother Clark please with all do respect, get out my way. I wish to leave your house with you alive."

She got even closer as she spat, "You can leave over my dead body."

"I wish you hadn't of said that."

With a swift move, I hit her in her chest. I know a punch like that will make your heartbeat irregular or go into a cardiac arrest. She stammered back and placed her hand on her chest. I glared at her and she stared blankly at me. Mother Clark fell.

I ran to the door and called out at Amanda, "Call 911."

The lady ran in her house, and I walked casually back to the old hag. Mother Clark is barely alive. Walking like an untouchable, I got beside her and laid her head in my lap. She was almost in an unconscious state. The old woman glared at me as if she wanted my help. I shook my head and whispered, "Go to Hell. You are an old nosey heifer, who deserves to die. And honestly, I never liked you; in fact, I can't stand you. I hope your granddaughter's boyfriend rapes her daughters and fucks her boys."

Mother Clark gave me stunned look as she took her last few breaths. I closed her old eyes and continued sitting there with her head in my lap.

Chapter 6

Amanda came over right before the paramedics. When she saw me, she saw a teary-eyed person holding the head of her dear friend. She got on the other side calling out, "Hang in there Mary. You hear me?"

I didn't tell her how her friend is already gone. I played along by calling out in a panic, "Can you still hear me Mother Clark? Open your eyes. Squeeze my hand. Do something."
The EMT's arrived and took her and her friend Amanda on the hospital. The police asked what happened and I told them she was doing fine and suddenly she grabbed her chest and fell. I ran to the door and called out for help. When they left, I went and called Houston. Feeling partially responsible, I drove towards the hospital. Houston finally picked up and said, "Let me guess? You forgot to stop by and I have to do it later."

"No, was there but I am on my way to the hospital."

"Hospital for what?"

"She grabbed her chest and fell out."
"Who!"

"Mother Clark. She was about to sign the check, but she fell out."

"She didn't sign it?"

I was puzzled. Mother Clark is a trusted tithe payer and a generous giver to this ministry. She is more than likely dead, and he is concerned about her signing the check. It didn't add up. I stated, "What did you say?"

"I mean what hospital is she in?"

"The EMT's have her on the way to the city hospital."

"I'm on my way."

We hung up. I started hitting my fist against my head. *Why couldn't I have controlled my temper when she came at me* I thought as I drove the speed limit? When I arrived, I saw her friend Amanda in the waiting room crying. The older woman wanted a hug. I hug her as she asked, "She was fine a few minutes ago. How can she be gone, now?"

"Life is a funny thing, and I know that just as much as anyone."

She cried more as she said, "Mary was like a sister."

I thought *she was like a nuisance to me* as I continued consoling Amanda. Houston arrived and came over. He asked, "Is she ok?"

Amanda was crying as I shook my head no. He looked angry more than hurt. Amanda stated between tears, "I'm glad we talked today before she passed on. I told her I loved her, and we hugged. I will never forget that."

"You got a chance to do what others wish they could do. You said goodbye and you didn't do it to an empty body. You talked and you made her laugh while she was still breathing. Be thankful for that."

She was drying her tears some as she shook her head in agreement. Houston was watching me consoling the grieving friend. I placed my hands on her shoulder and spoke, "I speak on behalf of Reeds Chapel U. L. M. we are sorry for your loss and if there is anything we can do for you and Mother Clark's family let us know. We are here to serve you and those you love."

"Thank you. I'm glad she was there with you. Have you come to get her body?"

"Not yet. The family isn't notified."

She shook her head and said, "I just can't believe she is gone. I can't believe she is not in the land of the living anymore."

"Go home and rest. Don't tire your body out, Mrs. Amanda. There isn't anything more you can do, and you can't do anything if you yourself become ill in some form."

"I will do that. Thank you for being here Bobby D. and you too Minister Houston."

"We are here for you if you need us, Mrs. Miles" Houston added.
She nodded and left. I asked, "I'm glad you came."

"You were good. I mean you really have a heart for those who lose a loved one. You had me wondering if you were a director or something."

"Every so often I come from the back and console a family because I must make sure their loved one is as close to life like as possible."

"You take pride in your work and I'm glad you work with us but what all happened?"

"She was about to sign the check, but she grabbed her chest and fell back."

"She didn't get a chance to sign it at all while you were there?"

"No, her friend, the lady you saw Mrs. Amanda came over and they chatted for the most. When she left, she grabbed her chest and fell."

I didn't like the way he was fishing for answers. I came out and asked, "She been going to the church for as long as I could remember and you aren't concerned about her dying. All you spoke of is if she signed the check or not."

"I am concerned."

Right now, is not the time to tell him what all she said about the check so I stated, "Has her next of kin been notified?"

"I called her granddaughter Tina. She is on her way because her mom dead."

"Sure is. I forgot. She died right before I left."

"Tina is the only kin other than Teona. You staying here and for the body or are will you wait until they call for you?"

Trying to decide, I was thinking as I spoke out loud, "I will give them time to grieve and let them call me at the funeral home; unless Inga is going to be there."

"She's at the house with the children. They can call you. Your mother is on her way."

"It's time for me to go."

"Bobby D. you can't avoid her."

"I know I can't but I won't talk to her; well not today."

"Go on. When I finish up here, I will go over to Mother Clark's and get the check."

"Ok. I'm heading home then back to the morgue and wait."

"Alright."

I left Houston and now I am curious about the bank statements and everything. I don't know why getting that unsigned check is up most important. I do plan on seeing what's on paper. I hadn't gotten a chance to check them out and from how he is acting, the old biddy might have been onto something. I headed to the hearse wagon as her daughter's family was coming in. Her granddaughter Tina saw me and asked, "They called you already?"

"No. I was there visiting her, when she went on to be with her God. I am deeply sorry for your loss, Tina."

"Thank you" was her uncaring reply.

As my memory served me well, Tina and her grandmother Mother Clark did not get along because Mother Clark was cutting her out the will if she didn't marry some trailer trash Mother Clark called him. Instead, Tina married for money and married some older man Mother Clark hooked her up with. To my memory, Tina was angry because the man she married was forcing her to have child.

She ended up having one and Teona, her one had four children with a boyfriend. I am not caring about all of them. I went back to the funeral home, and everyone was gone. I don't feel bad about doing that. I told her to let me out, but she wouldn't listen. I was in the military for seven years and for one year I did private jobs. The one thing I learned in the jungle is, you don't show any fear. You state your claim, and you act on it but as always you give warnings, and I did.

The old bat wouldn't listen, and I took actions upon my own. I even closed my eyes to recall how I told her to get out my personal space and how I have phobias of being too close to people and she wouldn't listen oh well. I went in the office and began researching the financial status of the ministry. I didn't see anything out of place at first until I probed deeper into the past finances. I saw how the money in the bank did not match the money that was taken out.

If you are just glancing, you would not see it because it is so easily to overlook it. I went a little further back and took into account how the ministry was indeed prospering while I was here. Since I been gone, I saw how the business had just enough money to stay afloat. Someone is stealing money and not taking small change either. I recalculated and did a lot of refiguring to see that every month the business is missing up to twenty thousand dollars. I noticed how the expenses were not adding up and to me the finger points to Inga, Houston and or my dad.

From what I can tell, my mother can't possible get her hands on this money. She is a show boat. She will buy all kinds of extravagant things and care not for the cost. Since I been here, I haven't seen her buy anything like that. So it can't be her as I first thought; although, the finger did point to her in my eyes. But it is Inga that collects all the money and her initials are clearly seen but it is my dad and Houston that states how it is spent; unless they have a business accountant that is doing some underhanded mess.

It doesn't make sense I thought as to why any of them would steal from the business if they are the primary people that get paid other than two or three more other people, excluding me. *Something's not right* I thought as I in my mind went back to the short time I had been here, none of them had any habits or attain anything of value. It's like the money is disappearing into thin air and that could be why Houston wanted me back so I could see what is going on but he hasn't showed me any expenses. I haven't asked either.

However, I saw how it seemed that the business paid for the vehicles, but I bought them myself and donated them to the business. *Someone could be hiding something from the IRS and me* I thought as I closed the statement book and put it back up. I left Inga's office and my cell rung. It was Houston. *Great* I thought as I spoke, "Hey."

"You still at the office?"

"Yeah. I been sitting here waiting on the family, but no one has called me yet."

"Here is the thing. You have the order to go get the body but do not do anything to it."

"Why? What is going on?"

"Since Mother Clark's was a widower, Tina is the next of kin and Tina wants her cremated within a day or two, but Tina's daughter Teona is planning on stopping it. You just have to go get the body and put her in the freezer."

I was blown away. I was sure Mother Clark was the type who'll want a big shin dig of a
Home Going Celebration but to hear Tina wants

her toasted was different. I replied, "Oh. Give me a few and I will be on my way."

"Ok. Remember don't touch it."

"I won't. It's just now right at four thirty and if I hurry up, I can finally make it to the grocery store."

"You still haven't been?"

"No."

I left out and headed to hospital. When I got there, Tina's daughter Teona was there and so was the police. They saw me and she came. She was furious with tears as she spoke softly, "Bobby D. please don't let my mom do this to my grandmother. You know her like I did. She would want a funeral."

The truth is I do know her, and I don't care either which way as long as I hurry up and leave. I know these people want sympathy so I gave them sympathy, "I am very truly sorry for your loss, and I am with you but if your mother is the primary next of kin, there may not be anything I could do about it."

"Hold off as long as you can. I plan an injunction."

I should laugh in her face because I want her toasted but I must pretend with a sorrowful in speech, "Your grandmother was one of a kind and she had her own way of doing things. I can understand your reasons for wanting her."

"My mom just mad. What if she was forced to marry my dad. We can't change that and her getting custody of my grandmother's body won't change a thing."

"I don't know about your family history" I stated.

"Yes, you do and you know I know you do. My family is just as much as a part of Reed's Chapel as you anyone alive or dead" she spat.

"I have orders and so far, your mother is the winner. Right file your injunction before I push the button. Once it is pushed I can't turn it off and if I did, you wouldn't want her body."

"You right and thank you Bobby D. for listening. I wasn't leaving until I saw who was coming for the body."

She walked off and before she could leave her mother Tina came over. I remember Tina quite well because my mom has called out so many demons in her. Mother Clark's daughter spoke with a demand, "I demand you give me information about my daughter's plan."

"She desired information about getting the body."

"She can ask all she wants. I am the first next of kin. I was the only child. All grandmother

Clark's sisters and brothers are dead. As for her nieces and nephews, I don't remember them for they are older. But it doesn't matter. I want her burned the day after tomorrow anyway."

I could tell Tina didn't have forgiveness in her heart. Then again, I am a fine one to talk, I haven't talked to my own mom, and I know I can't keep avoiding her. Tina said, "I know my mother was a piece of work and I know she would want the lavish funeral, but I won't grant her final wish. She should have changed her will, but she didn't. Just for that, I'm having it my way or at least, I will feel like I won the battle."

"I am sorry for your loss."

"Thank you, but Bobby D. try to understand I loved her in my own way. I am still harboring feelings of pain from being made to marry my daughter's dad when I didn't want his old ass just his money."

"It all came with the territory but look, it's now almost five and I must get your mother in our morgue and wait until one of you brings me orders. Mind you, we like to embalm her if that is the case soon as possible but if no funeral, it won't matter."

"I will let you know in the morning about the outcome."

I left Tina as I went to the hospital morgue. I showed my ID, and the loader helped me put her in the back of my hearse wagon. I looked in the rearview mirror and asked, "You ok back there?"

I didn't hear anything. I stated, "You must be fine. I didn't hear you say anything."

I drove off and made arrived at our funeral home. My dad was there. He helped me unload the body. We pushed her body to the embalming room and placed her in the sliding freezer table drawer after I tagged her. When I left out, I noticed how my dad hadn't said anything. We walked out back and locked up. Before I got in the hearse wagon, I stopped and asked, "What is it dad? You haven't said a thing, and I know something is up."

He walked over to me and stated flatly, "Your mother wants to see you when you get home."

"Must I go?"

He placed his hand on me and stated kindly, "Bobby D. you have to talk to her sooner than later especially now. She just lost a dear friend."

"You mean a dear tithe payer and butt kisser." He looked at me and I know he didn't like what I said. Quickly I apologized by saying, "I am sorry for those, array of words. She was a dear friend to my mother, and she ran the Mother Board with a stern hand. She always made sure all the programs were on time and worth watching. This ministry will surely miss her and there won't ever be another one like her."

I told the truth, but I didn't care. My dad said, "Thank you. I liked those array words better, but I let me talk for a moment."

"What is it to talk about?"

"My only child left and only shows back up because Houston asked. We are your parents, and we love you very much."

"I never said you didn't love me dad."

"Your mom loves you as well."

I didn't say a word because in a way, I believe it. How she feels about me never crossed my mind. It really makes me no never mind about it. I put it in my past and left it there but now I must face it and get it over with. Like it or not. My dad gave me his confident smile when he spoke, "Bobby whatever caused you to flee I am so sorry, but I am here for you. If it would help, I'm listening."

"Dad it is no secret I never liked the way momma missuses the church and their funds. I know she helped take care of me and Houston coming up but that is no excuse. She drank when no one was watching, she cursed behind closed doors, and had the nerve to want the church, hanging out at the Buzzards Hangout. How can she ever tell me about a call on my life when I see the call she says she has on hers? I told her I don't want a call on my life. I see how having a call can do you and I want no part of it."

"I understand your confusion as a young person, but your mother has good intentions. It is true she doesn't line up with the Word, but she tells the people the Word. It is up to them to follow up for themselves and not to watch her."

"She is in authority position. They will watch her."

"I know but we all shall work out our own soul salvation with fear and trembling. As for her drinking, I knew she was sneaking and drinking I just didn't say a word. I didn't know she was making you keep it from me and you felt torn by her dishonesty. I didn't know about any of that until you left and she told me. I blamed her for making you leave and later I asked for forgiveness. My child, she is a grown woman, and I can't raise her no more than she can raise me. I can only tell her about herself when no one is around but that was all I could do. I love her but she has to do what is best for her; just like you and me. The sad part is I know we pushed you too far and too hard, but we only want what is best for you. I am the first to admit we should have been better examples when we say we live for God, but we weren't. We talked a good game but when those doors closed, we were just as bigger sinners as the people we were leading. There are things I have done and still doing that I am not proud. My spirit is willing, but my flesh is weak; however, I am still a work in progress."

My head was bowed as I quietly allowed all he said to sink in. My dad said, "I need you to forgive me if it means anything."

I lifted my head up with surprise and quoted, "Forgive you for what? You didn't do as much damage to my faith as she did. Because of her, I refuse to hear a preacher talk about anything. I found myself in life, judging people for their sins because of the things I had gone through. As bad as I wanted to stop, I couldn't help it. I reject this so called "call" and I refused the Will of God."

"Bobby, my child hard not your heart. We were wrong for making make you walk in a calling you were not ready for. We saw then, like I do now you have an anointing on your life."

"Dad pleases! Not that again!"

"But it is true. If you are out the Will of God, you open bigger can of worms. I ask in good faith for forgiveness of the hurt and pain I have caused you throughout the years; when I could have stood up to your mom but didn't; times when I let her run over me and times when I let her think she had won. It became a time; I didn't want any arguing. I looked like a push over in your eyesight. It is for that; I am most hurt by."

I walked around the door and gave my dad a hug, I never knew he meant well, and I am glad he made me talk to him. Now I will go home and deal with my mother, the head strong warrior and get it over with.

Chapter 7

I drove the hearse towards home extremely slow. I am nervous and I shouldn't be. I turned into the driveway, and her study light was on. I knew she was up and waiting on me like my dad said. I have been back for over a month and talking to her is the last thing I have done. I don't have to worry about locking the door because no one is going to steal a hearse wagon.

When I opened the side door she was sitting in the living room. From her stance, she was waiting on me. My thoughts went everywhere but here. I wanted this to be as pleasant as possible so I spoke, "I am sorry about the loss of your friend."

My mother had old tears in her voice as she said, "Thank you for your condolence. I will truly miss Mother Clark."

I was about to walk past the living room where she was. With a clearer tone she called out, "Can you come in here for a spell? I need a word with you."

Without saying a word, I made my way towards her and sat down on the opposite side of the room. Up close the room reaped of cheap liquor and cigarette smoke. *She's smoking now* I thought as I turned up my nose. My mother opened her eyes and saw how distant I was. She didn't like it. She closed her eyes as she said, "You can sit closer. I don't bite. I am still your mother, Bobby D."

"It smells like smoke in here" I said as I got up fanning the air.

As if she was admitting it in a childish way, "I've been smoking."

"That's your new habit now?"

I stopped in front of the coffee table and picked up her cigarettes. I eased them in my jacket pocket. Right before she opened her eyes, she gave me a faint smile. I stood there listening to her saying, "I smoke after I eat, and I smoke to calm my nerves after those whiny church members come to me complaining about this and that. Those bastards have driven me to smoking and drinking."

"I'm surprise you're not popping pills or shooting up?"

"If they keep this up, who knows? I swear I am about to give up this preaching lifestyle. They have too many spirits for me to fight off every week."

"That goes with the territory but I thought you quit drinking?"

"I have slowed down some and at one point it was one glass a week."

I just stood there. She closed her eyes and said, "Sit down Bobby."

This time not to be disobedient, I sat on the edge of the small couch as she sat in the recliner near me. I waited for her as she talked with her eyes closed, "Bobby D. you have been staying here a few months, and you and I haven't talked."

"What is there to talk about? I am here to help get the business back on track. This is not a pleasure trip for me."

She opened her eyes and sat up in the recliner. Without smiling as usual her tone was, "Coming home should always be a pleasure trip but I have the strangest feeling you are dodging me?"

When she stated that, she closed her eyes again as to meditate. This time, she sat back and kept her eyes closed. I questioned her while making a statement, "Why would I do that? We are in the same house. We just live two different lives."

"I agree but you could make time for your parents."

"I see dad, and we talk daily."

My mother opened her eyes and said, "That's because you work in the business with him. Other than that, you might avoid him too."

"He wasn't the reason why I left and you know it."

"Do tell."

"Momma your dear church member just passed away. I should handle one thing at a time. We can talk later after Mother Clark is put to rest."

"I can multi-task besides I've waited on this conversation for over eight years. Why not now and get it out the way?"

"It's typical of you to make demands and expect all others to follow."

"I won't ask things of others I myself, won't do but I am sure you know that."

We both were quiet as I said, "Fine. Let us talk now. What you want to know?"

She opened her eyes and sat up like me. She searched me over as to get a grab on how I am but I didn't let my body language speak for me. She sat back and asked, "Was I that bad of a mother that you stayed away from me and quit serving the Lord?"

"Mother let me say this. Yes, you were a gracious mother but when it came to doing God's Will you were lousy. You would tell the church people one thing and do the very thing you tell them not too. You are a hypocrite in Jesus name. You make them do whatever it is you want and they would do it. Some have mortgaged their homes and lost them because of you and this church. You have

112

no compassion for God's people and as for me, you made me not want to serve HIM."

She sat up and this time she said, "Like I told you all those years ago. I tell them what the Word says and it is up to them to do it. They are not to do as I do but as I say. It is their fault if they don't search the scriptures for themselves. I have my own life and my own demons to fight. I have so many secrets that I always felt like I could trust you and that is why I always talked to you."

"You only talked to me because I was quiet and I wouldn't tell what you were doing behind closed doors."

"That and because you are trustworthy. I love you Bobby and to not have you serve God would crush me. I know you can be a powerful leader if you allow HIM to use you."

"Mother you don't get it and I don't think you ever will."

"What is there to get?"

"You really don't believe you have done any wrong to me."

"Seriously? I done you wrong? When all I ever done was to push you the right way. You are to thank me because I did you a favor."

"You didn't and please don't do me any more favors."

My mother was thinking of how to arrange her words. I know it because I know her. She spoke as to be on my level by affirming, "It never occurred I was in error. I was so sure you knew that I am in charge of my own life and everyone is in charge of theirs; that's why it never bothered me to tell you about the secrets you saw. It never occurred to me you would not walk in your purpose."

Tears were forming as I spoke, "All that talk about a call only pushed me away from God. I saw how you acted and swore not to ever be like that."

"How could I have done such a thing? I have only wanted what was best for you."

"Or best for you?"

"Either way my child, the best was coming. I didn't plan on you feeling like you do; especially, about God. You were my promise seed."

"What you mean, I was your promise seed?"

"You should of never known this but since the cat is looking out the bag, I might as well tell you."

"Tell me what?"

"You can't say anything."

"Mother tell me!" I literally screamed.

She took a deep breath and spoke, "Houston is my child by your uncle."

I was stunned, as I stared. After all these years I get it. Houston was the child she always dreamed of and I was an accident. He is more into the Word like her and he can be very persuasive if needed. I repeated, "Houston is not my cousin?"

"Oh, he is your cousin but your brother. He doesn't even know. Hell no one knows but me and now you."

"How could you cheat on my dad like that?" I asked with distaste.

"Let me tell you how."

I thought she and I were talking about how she made me the way I am but now I see there is a bigger picture. I dried up my eyes as she said, "All of this was before your dad, but let me start from the beginning. I was seeing your Uncle Paul and I didn't know he was married to Marie, until I found out I was pregnant with Houston. Your Uncle Paul went away in the war. While he was gone, his wife Marie found out about me. She lied to Paul about being pregnant because she found out she was sterile. She also said me having the baby was a God send to her. I told Paul I was not pregnant. Then she told Paul she was pregnant. When I had Houston for her, she died. When your Uncle Paul came home, I told him she left the baby with me. He allowed me to raise Houston because I got saved. I believed it was a Christian duty of mine by letting him hold onto the only child he and his wife had. It worked until he started drinking blaming Houston for his wife's death. I left

and wanted to take Houston but if I did, I would
have uncovered Marie's secret. Years went by and I
was on a church mission in Europe. Here I met your
dad. They didn't look nor act alike. I didn't know
they were brothers until we arrived back in The
United States as husband and wife. He didn't call
Paul by his name. He called him a nickname.
Anyway, Paul and I discussed telling your dad
but we didn't. To this day, neither he nor Houston
knows."

      I just sat there. I could not believe what I
was hearing from my mother. I asked, "That's when
Houston came to live with us?"

      "Yes. Paul was being cruel
to Houston. I encouraged Paul to let us raise him
and he agreed. Later he died and so did everything
until now."

      "Why are you telling me this?"

      "Bobby my child, you are trustworthy and I
for some reason find myself telling you my secrets."

      "Does my dad know now?"

      "No. We kept it from him. It would rip him to
pieces if he knew I was screwing his favorite
brother before I came to the Lord and had a baby. I
could not do that to your dad. I just couldn't."

      Just then we both heard my dad pull up. He
turned the lights off. She coyly said, "Remember
our secret."

I was going in my sleeping area as my dad came in. I stopped in the door. He saw me leaving out and asked, "No need to rush off on my account. I can leave you two alone if you need more time."

"I was finished."

"I hope you both got whatever it is off your chest and out this house."
She glanced at me and I said, "We did. It was more than I thought. Isn't that right mother?"

"Yes. Bobby is correct."

"Where you about to go?" my dad asked.

"Back to the funeral home. I like those people better."
My mother started laughing as she said, "Your sense of humor is ridiculous."

I went in the room packed a small bag and left back out. When I got there Inga was leaving. I pulled up beside her and asked, "Why you here, so late?"

"Houston got on my nerves, so I had to leave. I needed some me time and this is a perfect place for it."

"I wouldn't have thought about you being here, either."

"Why you here?" she asked in a surprise.

"Had an eye-opening conversation with my mom and I decided that I would rather be around the dead than the living."

She laughed as she said, "I don't agree with that but ok. Good night."

"Bye."

Inga drove off as I unlocked the door, went inside and turned off the alarm. I reset the alarm and lock the door back. I looked for anything to be out of place and so far, nothing. I went up front and checked in her office. It was clean as always. I sat in her chair and looked in the books. Everything was accountable until I saw a difference. The funeral home profited eighty thousand dollars at the beginning of the month and now it's at the end and there's only sixty-five thousand accountable for; that's fifteen thousand dollars in unanswered funds.

I went back over it and came out with the same numbers. *It doesn't make sense* I thought. If you scan over the numbers, you would not catch it. I caught it because it didn't look right. I will have to tell Houston about this. When I thought about him, I sat back in Inga's chair and became lost in thought. Here I am thinking I was the only child of my mother's, and I really wasn't. Throughout all the years, Houston has always been the brother I never had; in fact, he was the brother I always had. If I compared, he and my mom, I can see my mother all over him.

On the other hand, I can see my Uncle Paul in him. I yarned and put the books away. Feeling tired, I turned off her light and went to the small twin bedroom. I opened the door to a funny smell. It came to me a rat had died, and the scent wasn't quite gone. I made up the bed and got in it. Staring at the ceiling has been a past time for me and that was all I remember for somehow sleep found me. The next morning, I heard crying coming from Inga's office. I put my jacket on, closed the room door and went her way. I eased open the door and saw her head on the desk crying away. I asked sincerely, "What's wrong?"

She lifted her head. Her eyes were puffy and red. I sat across from her as she spoke between sniffles, "I knew we live in a cruel world but some people need to die and leave the rest of us alone."

"What happened?" I asked for my mind was thinking of Houston or one of her children.

"A friend of mine was having an affair with this married man."

I already didn't like it when she said that. Inga saw my demeanor changed and stated, "Let me finish before you judge her."

"Just one question."

"What?"

"Why didn't you tell her it was wrong?"

"How do you know I didn't tell her it was wrong?"

"Most of the time people say they are your friend but they don't give you the advice you need to hear. They will tell you what you want to hear."

"Just hear me out."

"Ok."

"When she told me about him, she was already in love. It had started off as a hit it and quit it. But she was sucking on him and he started spending all his time with her. He took loving care of her and she believed he felt the same way."

"What did you tell her? Because you know if we don't give Godly advice you, me us or whoever is just as at fault as the person that came to you for advice. Now, what did you tell her?"

"I told her she is grown and if that is what she wanted that it was on her."

"You didn't tell her it was wrong?" I questioned her.

"How was it wrong if he is seeing, talking and texting her all the time. He was just as guilty as she was."

"He is but when she came for advice you should have told her to leave him alone because there is no future in loving a married man or a taken man."

"I told her will give into account for her role in his marriage. My friend didn't care. If his wife cared, she would of be there for him and not be busy all the time. His wife is a traveling nurse and sometimes she is gone all the time; leaving him alone."

"Does he work?"

"He did but he lost his job from being downsized so his wife took the traveling nurse job to make up for the lifestyle he was used to living. He didn't want to travel with her so he stayed behind and that is when he met my friend."

I could tell if I be completely honest, Inga would not tell me the story. I put an apology in my mouth nicely, "I'm sorry. I just don't like adultery. It hurts more than the people that commit the sin. I won't judge. I'm listening."

"Thank you. A friend of mine was having an affair with this married man. During this time, he supposed to have left his wife but he changed his mind. He claims his marriage was more important than being with her. That was too late. She was already pregnant. He told his wife and they decided on a blood test after the baby was born. In the meantime, he was to have no contact with my friend. Whenever she called him, he treated her badly. He talked about her like a dog to anyone who listened. This married man made my friend look stupid for being in love with him. His wife acted like her husband was not at fault for anything. Anyway, the baby came three months early, weighing one pound and one ounce. The baby is in the NICU; you know the neonatal intensive care unit."

"Yeah, I know what it is."

"My friend delivered the baby at a different hospital because the man wife usually works at it. Come to find out his wife was an on-call nurse there, last night. She stole the baby and made a recording."

"Made a recording?"

Inga held her head down and cried harder. I sat there not knowing how to comfort her. To me, her friend should have investigated the man so there wouldn't be any room for mistakes. I don't understand how she didn't know he was married because whenever a woman starts seeing a man, she always finds out all she can about him. I believe her friend knew he was married and didn't care because of her feelings towards the man. Inga, lifted her head to say, "Oh Bobby D. the recoding tore my friend to pieces."

"What was on it?"

"The wife of this man stole the barely alive baby out the hospital. Somehow, she took the baby to a ball field."

Inga cried as she said, "Oh Bobby D. it was horrible."

"Take your time and tell me."

"She used her iPhone to demonstrate her pain. You could see her loading a cart full of boy's hard balls in the ball shooter; with one hundred miles per hour speed. She placed the baby girl near her iPhone. You could see the hand with the mitten on. This monster walked over and took the little girl in her hand. She placed the baby in a catcher's mitten as she squatted behind home plate. She caught the balls with the baby in the glove. I never saw so much blood and membrane splatting everywhere. You could hear the screams of the baby; while she laughed. After the third ball hit the glove, the baby stopped crying but she didn't stop there. This evil woman kept catching the balls one after the other until the ball shooter was empty. She intentionally killed the baby. SHE KILLED THE INNOCNET BABY!"

I thought, *it is sad, but the child was not innocent, not in my eyes. If the mother had done her job and not had premarital sex than her premature child would not have been subjected to such cruelty. I admit, it was harsh because it was aimed at a child, but sin is sin, and* **the Word says the wages of sin is death**. *The mother should have thought* *about her actions; if she had, the wife would not have been overcome with evil to do what she did. In truthfulness, I don't have a heart when it comes to sinners, who willingly and knowingly know what they are doing. I cannot in truth say I feel sorry for the woman that lost the child. Whether or not, she understands but the* **sin the parents do, and will; fall to the children if the curse is not broken according to the Word.** *I know the child did not ask to be born but it did not ask for the parents to do what they did. If the parents were living Godly, this would not be an issue but they weren't. Nevertheless, the baby is gone.* Inga stated, "When she got finished, she opened the mitten and you could barely tell there was a baby there. She pointed towards the iPhone and said, "Let this be a lesson to all you unfaithful people who knowingly have affairs that involves a love child."

      I was quiet as Inga told me, "Bobby D. she was born in the church."

      "Who was?"

      "His wife. She served as the Sunday school teacher of the seven-year old's. How could someone be in church do such a hideous crime? What kind of God did she serve, Bobby D.? That child was all my friend had and it tore her apart."

I didn't say a word because I was not bothered by what she said; just wish I had come up with that, when I was doing private jobs for people. Inga said, "You know what she said to the police when they arrested her?"

"No, what she say to the police?"

"She said they made her that way. She honestly believes my friend and her husband made her commit such a crime."

"As harsh as it sounds, the wife could be right."

"HOW! She killed my friend's baby."

"You want the truth or not?"

"Go on and tell me your opinion."

"She more than likely was giving her all to her husband. He is not a boyfriend but a husband she swore to love and protect in front of God. I admit, she didn't have to record it however, the child didn't ask for its parents to be liars or cheaters either. You know the sin of the parents will fall to the child. I'm not saying what the parents do will hurt the children but if the man and woman is not living for God and they don't teach their children about sin; then yes, a child can live what they saw. If they saw their parents doing all kinds of mess, they could end up doing it too because of what they were raised seeing. In this way, the sin of the parents can and will be passed on to the child if that child does not find Christ."

"Bobby D. the bad part is I know that. I can't see past the part that she made those balls hit the baby over and over. She could have stopped after the baby died but she didn't."

"She could have. Her husband and your friend could have stopped too but no one did."

"It was too late. She was pregnant then."

"If he was truly ignoring her and your friend must have done something to provoke the wife."

Inga thought before stating, "Now a few months ago, my friend kept calling their house and they told her to stop. My friend said the wife told her to leave them alone. My friend said she told the wife, all she wanted was her husband to talk to her but he refused."

"Then she should have obeyed their or her wishes. If he didn't want to talk to her she should have left it alone."

Inga was taking up for her friend in my eyes as she spoke with harsh words, "He is the daddy, and he should help take care of her needs. She didn't get the baby alone."

"No, she didn't but the wife and the husband asked her to leave them alone. The "baby daddy" wouldn't talk to her but your friend, kept at them right?"

"Yeah but."

"No, but's. She could have left them alone and after the baby was born; do a test like the wife said. Your friend still wanted her husband; I can tell you that is what it was. I've seen it too many times. Plus, you yourself said she didn't tell you until she fell in love."

"What's wrong with wanting to be with the man you got your baby by?"

"Everything is wrong if he is married and told you to leave them alone."

"You sound like Houston. He was telling me the same thing."

"Your husband was right. Look, I know it was a terrible thing done but sometimes parents and those you love can push you and push you. Before you know it, you'll snap."

"Just because I understand it; doesn't mean I like it."

Chapter 8

I left out of Inga's office and went to the Morgue. I sat in my seat and became engrossed in the conversation. I know how that wife felt about being pushed too far. I could understand the pain Inga was feeling; even though I am not married nor had affairs. Pain is pain and sometimes pain will make you do things you normally wouldn't do. I hit my jacket pocket, and I felt my mother's cigarettes.

Taking the pack of smokes, I laid them out one by one on the counter under the small heating lamp. I had a devilish grin about what I am going to do with them. I carefully put on my gloves, goggles and mouth mask. I turned on my trusted embalming machine and lightly sprayed all her cancer sticks with real cancer-causing material. I turned off the machine and put the gloves, goggles and the mask on the counter. I turned the lamp on so the cigarettes could dry very fast. While my back was turned, I heard a knock. I covered the sticks before yelling out, "Come in." It was Houston. I stared at him in a new way. Just seeing him didn't make me mad but made me wonder if he really didn't know. I discarded my thoughts as he said, "Can we talk?"

"Yeah, no one in here would mind."

Houston laughed as he walked in. He sat on the rolling chair. I asked, "What's on your mind?"

"I have a few things to discuss with you."

"I'm listening."

"First, I am glad you and your mom talked."

"How you know that?"

"Auntie called me and told me about it."

"Oh. What else did she say?"

"Nothing much, other than you ran off last night to come here."

"I did. The dead is better than the living."

He gave me a smirk as he said, "Did you see Inga here last night when you got here?"

"She was leaving as I pulled up."

"Who else was here?"

"Let me see, Mother Clark and the other two stiffs that has slow moving families."

Houston laughed. I don't know what he is getting at as I said, "Inga was here crying."

"Yeah, her friend lost her child."

"How you feel about that?" I asked.

"Well, I hate the child paid the ultimate price and it is always sad when a child's life is lost due to that nature."

"Was there something else you wanted to discuss?"

"Yes. You have to go to the city hospital and pick up the remains of the child and cremate it."

"From what Inga was telling me, it doesn't sound like there is much left."

"There isn't. The mother wants that done because she can't have an open casket for those to see her baby."

"Ok. Where's the paperwork?"

"It's up front."

"Could you bring it? I have to wrap this up."

"Yeah, let me go get them for you."

Houston left out. I put the gloves on and mask on as I placed each cigarette back in the box. I even sealed the boxes with a special seal that looked store bought. I put the boxes of smokes back in my jacket pocket as Houston came in and said, "Here you go. The mother wants it done today" as he handed me the paper.

"That shouldn't be a problem" I stated as I placed the paper in my hand.

"Where are my parents?"

"Your dad is in the county taking up burial and your mother is visiting Tina, at Mother Clark's house."

"Have they decided when the funeral will be?"

"That's the thing. Your mother is furious because Tina wants to cremate Mother Clark; while, Tina's daughter Teona wants a funeral on Saturday; the last day of this month."

"My mother has nothing to do with it and that's a few days from now."

"I know."

"I haven't done anything to the body and do you know how hard it's going to be just to get blood out of her and loosen up her old skin? Her body is going to look gray because of her age and how long it is taking them."

"We know; they don't."

My first thought was, Mother Clark is going to burn on earth, then burn in Hell; what a terrible way to be dead. I asked, "Who has the rights?"

"The lawyer says Tina does because she is the next of kin but her daughter Teona is the legal heir to all Mother Clark's things."

"Then why is her daughter going against her mother? She is getting all her money and property. I mean to include all my mother doesn't get at least."

"You knew Mother Clark like I knew her. She would rather have an all-out expense paid funeral for everyone to come and see her; decked out."

"True, but if Tina brings in proof about the cremation, its grilling time for Mother Clark."

"Bobby D. you have a way with words."

"In this line of business, you have too."

"I need you to do something for me."

"If I can. What you need?"

"I need you to be the God Parent to my sons if anything happens to Inga or me."

I was stunned. A God Parent? I am not even a parent, period. I asked, "You want me to be the God Parent to your boys if something happens to you and Inga?"

"Yes. Will you consider it?"

"What does Inga say?"

"She liked the idea. We believe you will be a great parent if the time comes. Would you do it?"

This is huge and for him to ask it of me, must means he thinks a lot of me. With a smile I replied, "Yes. I will do it."

"Great! We had already placed it in our will."

"How did you know I would have said yes?"

"I didn't but God did. Well get on over and get the little one."

"Ok. Let me get the small body bag."

I got the body bag and went to the hearse. I got in and left out. I made a stop at my parent's house. I went inside and placed my mom's cigarettes back on the end table where I found them. I left out to go get the baby. When I got to the hospital, I showed the attendant the paper and they released the body to me. The baby body bag was too big but I had to make it do.

I went back to the morgue and eagerly opened the bag. All I could see was a ball of small bones, tissue fragments, blood and what resembled a frame of a baby. The face was not recognizable. There was nothing to really burn. I made my notes and went to the furnace outside. I turned it on to one thousand degrees. I went back inside and waited for ten minutes. I didn't need to wait long but to do things right; I waited. When the ten minutes were up, I went to the furnace and pulled out the steel rolling bed. I placed the baby on the rack, pushed it back in and started the burning process.

This will be over soon I said within myself as the burning of the lifeless baby began. A knock was heard at the door. I went to the door and saw Inga. I stepped outside and asked, "What is it?"

"I was just checking to see if you were finished with the baby."

"I just put the baby in. I'm sure it won't be long. Does the mother have an urn she wants to use or does she want the one we provide?"

"She has one and I left it out front. I'll be back with it."

She left and I went back inside. The little baby was no more than a heap of ashes. I turned off the furnace. I took the baby out and set the cooling timer as I waited for Inga to come back. She came back and knocked on the door. I stepped outside and got the urn. It was very pretty and unique. I asked, "Where she got this from? It is very nice."

"I forgot where she said she got it from but it is pretty."

"Is she going to keep it or take it to a private place?"

"She wants to keep it then let it go."

"Oh. Ok. In about thirty minutes come back with the paperwork for me to sign and her mother can come get it."

"Ok."

I went inside and checked on the cooling remains. I stepped back outside where Inga was still waiting. I said, "You know in some cases, I could have allowed the mother to push the button to start the process, but I thought I would have been too much for her."

"It would have been ok but thanks for the thought."

"When is the mother coming by?"

"Soon as I give her the call, which, I am about to do in a few."

"Have they decided on what they are going to do about Mother Clark? She is taking up space if she's not going to be embalmed."

"We should know something at any minute." Just then the timer went off and I said, "Ok. Let me go and bring you out the remains."

I left Inga waiting as I went inside and poured the remains in the urn. I even added a little ash to make it fuller because if I left it like it was, she would have had nothing. I brought the small urn back and Inga said, "I am still at a loss of words."

"What did the daddy say about all of this?"

"To my knowledge he hadn't really said anything about it but he did call my friend. He told her he was sorry for the loss, and he hopes she can put it pass her in time. That was inconsiderate and thoughtless."

"How?"

"His wife did this to her and he wants her to put it pass her and go on."

"He was clearly saying, he hopes she can move on and not let it stop her from living."

"Then he should have said that."

"Men have a weird way of saying things. You should know that more than anyone; you're married to a minister."

"But still. He could have said something better than that."

"Your friend is lucky he said that. Most men would have probably kept their words to themselves and let it ride. To a lot of them, the problem is over."

"Yeah, but I hope his wife rots in Hell."
I did not like the way she was defending her friend. I know it is her friend but what about the marital strain her friend helped place on the wife. *I don't*

think she has any idea what pain was being caused by this three-way love affair I thought. As nicely as possible I made this statement, "If that is the case, your friend and that woman's husband should meet her there because they all played a role in the dying of this child. Your friend and that husband are not innocent. They put their selfish needs ahead of doing the right thing, ahead of his marriage and ahead of the possibility of getting pregnant, which did occur."

"I didn't say they were" Inga said with a sharp tone.

"No, you didn't but you only look at the fact that, a wife killed her husband's love child. A man committed an affair with a single woman, which, I believe knew he was married but she kept the affair. I also believe he told her he was not going to leave his wife, and she trapped him by getting pregnant, but that did not work. It backfired. Now look at the mess that happened all because of dick and pussy couldn't do right."

Inga was silent as she listened. I know she knows I am telling the truth, but it made me no difference, I as I said, "I have seen things like this happen all the time. There's nothing you can say to convince me, that your friend did not know he was married. I bet she knew but she was so in love that she wanted him from his wife. It is only then she

136

decided to trap him by getting pregnant, but none thought about the grieving wife; by the way formed issues of her own. Who knows? She probably thought she could not take the idea of her husband fathering a child outside of her marriage. Some women who are brought up in church, believes it is like an ultimate sin; when a love child is produced. Then deal with the affair, then with a child. Who knows what all he may have told his wife about your friend? My thing is, if she rots in Hell, they need to meet her there because they all are guilty; they just didn't physically do the killing act of the baby."

"It makes sense Bobby D. but to kill a baby?"

"I know; but go call the mother so she can come by. Her urn is ready."

Inga left and I was glad. I got tired of her defending the guilty. I told her the truth and she acted like the world. She could only see the cause but not the effect. I hope the lady doesn't get to serve as much time as the people aim for. She should get time but not as they want. Houston came back as I was walking back inside. I paused as he said, "We got the court order."

"What court order?"

"Tina won and she wants to hurry up and cremate her."

"When?"

"She is on her way. She wants to push the button."

"Tina is in the right, right?"

"Yes. You know I will make sure of that."

"Ok. Let's bring her out as we wait for Tina."

Houston and I fetched Mother Clark's body. The naked body was indeed dark, gray and dead. We covered her up as we rolled her inside the crematoria. I turned the furnace on. Houston said, "You been using this today?"

"Yeah, I just did Inga's friend's baby."

"Sure did. I didn't know you were on it that fast."

"I like to do my job, quickly but effectively."

"I see you do."

We laughed. Tina came to the door and knocked. Inga was with her as we came outside. I asked, "Allow me to see the papers for myself."

"I have them already in file" Houston said.

"Still I would like to see them."

"I will go get them" Inga said as she scurried off.

"You sure you want to do this?"

"I am very sure" Tina said as she waited for Inga.

Inga returned and gave me the papers. I checked them over and they were in order. I handed them back to Inga and asked, "You want to push the button?"

"Yes. I want to make sure she's toast."
I glanced at her and she stated, "It's no secret we didn't get along after I married the man she wanted me too."

"That is none of my affair" I stated.

"Mine either" Houston stated.

"Now that is out the way, let's get this over with."

The three of us, stepped in the small building. There on the rack was Mother Clark. Tina asked, "Can I say few words?"

"This is your grieving time. Do as you wish."
Tina walked in front of the furnace door and placed her hands on the button. She said, "I wish you were alive to hear me say this but who cares as long as I get a chance to tell you. I loved you and the day you made me marry that man was the day I
started hating you. You made me this way. You made me hate when I wanted to love. You made me angry at you and at God but now I have closure and an inner peace. I hope you burn on earth, as you do in Hell."
Tina pushed the button and flames covered Mother Clark's body. She walked off and said, "Let me know when she is finished."

Houston and I looked at her as she closed the door. I stated, "Wow."

"I know."

We left out so the furnace could do her thing. When we came outside Tina was still there as she asked, "It's over already?"

"No, but give it a little while. Mother Clark was a medium size woman."

Houston stated, "Let me get back in front. He will have to put her in the back burner."

"Go on. I will be out here."

I faced Tina and asked, "What kind of urn you want to put her in?"

"The cheapest you have."

"Go around front and enter that way. Get with Inga or Houston. They will show you want you are asking. I am going to wait out here until the process is complete."

Tina walked back out front and I was there waiting. I smiled because I liked the way Tina was being honest in how she was feeling. Some people will tell lies and preach a person into heaven; knowing they were the devils themselves if not worse. I liked the fact how Tina was finally getting some things off her chest; although, she said them to an empty shell.

About thirty minutes had passed as Mother Clark was in the back burner. Here comes Teona. She was running with papers up high. She yelled, "Is it too late! I have the injunction papers."

"I'm sorry but it is too late. She is in the back burner."

Teona broke down and cried. I wanted to console her but I didn't like her grandmother that much. I knew I should have compassion. I squatted with her and said, "I'm so sorry."

Teona was crying too hard to hear me. She kept saying, "Mother could have given me the body for a funeral. She could have."

"It will be ok."

"Bobby D. she knew what she was doing. She knew a funeral would mean the world to my grandmother. My mother is a hateful bitch. I hate her! I hate her!"

"Don't hate her. You don't want hate to bloom in your life and your heart. You don't want to be like her if you say she has hatred."

The young girl kept crying. Houston came outback. He saw her and asked, "Is everything ok?"

"No. Teona just brought the papers to stop the cremation, but it was too late."

"Bobby D. is right. It was too late. Is there anything we can do?"

"No, there is nothing you or this funeral home can do."

Houston helped her up off the ground as I stood up. The grieving young woman stated proudly, "I get the ashes."

Houston read the paper. It stated just as she said. Houston asked, "You have an urn?"

"No. I will bring one back."

"We have quite a few selections, if you want to see them."

"I do. I want the best money can buy."

"Come this way."

Before they could make it around the corner, Tina came and questioned, "What is she doing here?"

"She brought injunction papers, but the cremation process had already been completed."

"So, she was late?" her mother asked in a happy way.

"Yes, but the papers say she gets the remains."

"No, the hell they don't."

"Mother you won. You had her cremated and I wanted a funeral because we both knew she would have wanted it. Let me have the remains as the papers state."

"I intend to put the old dictator in the ocean."

"Mother let me have a small ceremony for her friends to tell her goodbye."

"I'm sorry Tina but they do say she gets the remains" Houston added.

"We'll see about that" Tina said as she stormed off.

Houston and Teona went on around front. I went back inside and turned off the furnace. The old nosey hag is not a heap of ashes. Houston came in and handed me one of the most expensive urns money could buy. Houston looked at me and said, "Hurry up. I want Teona to have it before her mother denies her the right to have a funeral for her."

In haste, I poured Mother Clark in the urn and Houston took it to Teona. I cleaned up the area and dipped a new pack of my mother's smokes in the secret ingredient. *I can't wait to see how she is going to act with all her smokes laced with the finest chemicals we have here* I thought.

Once they dried, I placed them back in the pack and called it the day.

When I got home, my mom was still gone. I placed her smokes on the end table and headed to open room. I took a bath and sat on the day bed. I wanted to watch TV but nothing was on. I got up and turned the light off. I lay back down and stared at the ceiling. I thought about how I still couldn't get my mother to see how she was a part of my problem. No matter how I told her, she was in denial. She thinks she had nothing to do with me and the way I am.

At least my dad owned up to his small part in my upbringing and lack of faith. At least he wants to make it right and better between he and I but something doesn't add up. I don't understand what is really going on because Houston questioned me about seeing Inga at the funeral home and my mother now states she is his mother; but he does not know. My father doesn't even know or so she claims.

Nine out of ten if she only told me then she is telling the truth. I just don't get it how she finds a way to tell me of her secrets. I don't know if she knows that I won't tell or she just assumes because I don't talk to anyone outside of the funeral home. I don't even go to her church. Before I listen to her spew lies, I go to the funeral home and read or stay all day doing nothing. I refuse to partake in her mess when I have stuff I have to pay for.

"Bobby D. wake up."

I turned over and wiped my face. When did I fall asleep? I thought as I heard it again, *"Bobby D. wake up."*

Something did not feel right when I heard my name. The very echo of my name made me alert. It sounded like the voice I heard in the hotel room a few months ago right when Houston called. This time, I sat up to get a better view. There in the corner was a very tall figurine. This spirit stood to

144

the ceiling. Its body span was not human at all; for it was about four feet wide. It wasn't a fat person but a healthy-looking being. The very sight of this would make the average person quiver and call on the name of their God but not me.

I know this can't be real because no human being is as wide or that tall. However, I kept quiet and kept looking because messenger had on an all-black robe that covered the top of the head and feet. The right hand had on a white glove and in that gloved hand was a long thick staff of some sort. I leaned a little closer and the dark model used its left hand to show its face. I shook my head to clear up my view; for its face was completely black with piercing eyes. The mouth had a blacker straight line with no nose. *I must be dreaming* I thought as I wiped my eyes again.

The tall statue was still there. I sat there staring. I stretched my neck and eyes to make sure someone was in the corner. Indeed, someone or thing was in the corner. I didn't say a word as the figment of my imagination stated in a slow dragging tone that makes your soul shake, *"Bobby D."*

Now I know I am not seeing or hearing things. I spoke, "Huh? Who are you? What you want with me?"

It came to mind, how some people believe in the Death Angel. Come to think of it; this is what it must be. Immediately I thought *I was about to die and be a cadaver for someone to work on; like I had done many others.* Oddly enough, I was not afraid. The tall character spoke again and this time, I heard as clear as a summer's day, *"A work to do from the time, it takes to conceive until the time it takes to give birth: 9 months."*

Just like that, it vanished before my eyes. Sweat began pouring off me and my breathing became raspy. I'm having a panic attack. Luckily, I'm familiar with the signs as I breathe in and out slowly. Soon as my breathing became normal, I went to sleep and when I woke up. I noticed it was four o'clock.

August
Chapter 9

This is how my first day of August is going to be like I thought as I went towards the kitchen for some water. I saw my mother had taken her extra cancer smokes off the end table, but I paid it no mind. I was thirsty. *This is going to be good* I thought. I stood at the sink and filled a glass of water. The liquid was cool and felt wonderful going down my throat. Soon as I turned around, I saw my mother. She didn't see me, but I continued to stand there. When she did see me, she jumped and yelled, "Don't scare me like that!"

"I'm sorry mom. I wanted some water."
I moved out of her way as she walked over and fixed her some water. She asked, "You couldn't sleep?"

"No. You?"

"Not really. I been bothered by the fighting Tina and Teona were doing over the remains of Mother Clark."

She drank some water and lit a cigarette. She took a puff and looked at it. I asked, "Is it ok if I sit over here. The smell bothers me."

"Sure."

In truth, I know of the little something extra and didn't want to smell it. She puffed and puffed

147

on the cigarette. I kept my thoughts in my head as she said, "Teona has the remains, and she plans on having a small ceremony. Are you coming?"

"If I am not busy."

"Make time. I'm sure Mother Clark would love to have you there."

I said within, *I'm sure Mother Clark would love to have some water too; where she is at now,* but I stated, "I guess I can make it."

"Great. The small gathering will take place today."

"At the church?"

"Where else Bobby?"

"At what time?"

"It's set for one."

I didn't answer as she lit another cigarette. I got up and went back bed thinking *about the IT I saw in the corner. The way it said I had nine months, but I don't know for what? What work should be occurring while I am here? What is this thing that comes to me?* I will ask Houston what he thinks when I see him today. As of right now, I plan on sleeping harder than I did before.

A few hours passed and I woke up. I got dressed and left the house with my sights on the funeral home. When I got there, my dad was talking to Inga, and he seemed upset. They seemed to be yelling but almost immediately it stopped when they saw me. Inga went back in through the back door and my dad ran his fingers though his black and white hair. I turned the car off and locked the doors. My dad did not look at me as I asked, "What's going on here?"

"Nothing Bobby."

"It didn't look like nothing to me. You two were yelling or something."

"I said it's nothing. She has to do her job."

"Oh. Houston here yet?"

"Yeah, he's in his office. When you go in tell him I'll be back I have to run an errand."

"Ok."

He walked off rapidly and got in his old truck. I know those two are hiding something about the business, but I don't know what. I went in the back door and headed to Houston's office. When I got to the end of the hall, I heard Inga say, "You are so involved in this business that you don't see your family business going down the drain."

"I am a man of God. I know I have been estranged from you and the boys, but I must figure out where the funeral home money is going. If you know something you need to tell me. I don't want us to get audited and then out of business. If we go out of business, we are without a job. If I am without a job, I can't do my job as a family man."

"I don't know where the money is going to Houston. I log everything in, and I deposit what I have on paper."

"If you do then how is it, the business is missing so much money at the end of every quarter?"

"I don't know. I swear I don't know."

"Well, somebody around here knows something I don't."

"Maybe the dead are coming back and recollecting their money from us" Inga said to make herself laugh.

"This is not a joke. Do you have a hidden habit you are not telling me?"

"Are you for real? I am your wife, and my day involves this business and the children."

"Yes, I am for real. How do you think it looks, if my wife is stealing money from the business I work at?"

"If I am stealing money from this business, then why is the church money still accounted for? If I were stealing, wouldn't I steal in every aspect?" He was quiet. I thought she was right. Now I am thinking maybe she isn't stealing money because she seems so sincere. I have been thinking my dad had something to do with it until she said, "I tried telling Lee the same thing. I told him I love you all and wouldn't jeopardize anything. He was mad and we started yelling until Bobby D. pulled up."

"Let me think as I talk to Bobby D."
She was heading towards her office. I closed the casket room door as an indication that I was in the building. I made it to the end of the hall and Inga saw me. She smiled pleasantly, "Good morning."

"Good morning. Is your husband here?"

Inga smiled a carefree smile as she stated, "He's in his office doing business as usual."
I let her walk by as I made my way to his office. When I got there, Houston was sitting there looking more like my mother than anything. I ignored the likeness and gave the door a light knock. He glanced at me and smiled. I stated, "Dad, I mean my dad said he was gone on an errand. I guess he will be back in the office today; although, he did not indicate it."

"Ok. What's up with you this day?"
While standing in his door, I stated "I need to talk if it's ok or if you have time?"

"I always have time to talk to you if you need me. Come on in and have a seat."
I walked in and he said, "Close the door."

I closed the door and sat opposite of him. I said, "Do you believe in the death angel?"
Houston sat back and stared at me in a wondering way. He is trying to read my expression. I made

sure it showed nothing. Houston got up and walked around me to his door. I turned my head to see what he was about to do. He called out, "Inga! Inga!"
She trotted to her door and said, "What's wrong?"

"Hold all my calls. Bobby D. is in here with me and I don't want to be disturbed unless it is God HIMSELF."

"Ok."

He came back in and closed his door. He sat down and asked, "You had a visitation, didn't you?"

"I'm not going to say it was a visitation."

"What you want to call it?"

"I don't know."

"What did it say?"

"It started about the beginning of June."

"You were here since then."

"No. It started the day you called me; which, was the beginning of June."

"You right. Keep going. I won't interrupt."

"My plane got delayed and I was on my way to Thule. When I got to the hotel, I was almost asleep when I heard nine months. A work to do; nine months."

Houston stared at me as if he was amazed. I continued my remembering of the past accounts by saying, "Then last night or early this morning, I heard it again; except this time, I saw it. The vision I saw was a shadow that called my name and told me to wake up. I woke up, looked around and sat up. Then I saw the thing in the corner. Houston, I knew it wasn't real because it reached the ceiling, and it was about four feet wide. The thing had on all black robe on. It covered the head and the feet. I guess it had feet but I wasn't looking. All I know is the robe was very long. The messenger, I say, had a white glove on its hand with some type of staff or stick. The face was completely black with piercing eyes. The mouth had a blacker straight line with no nose."

"Yes, I know exactly what you are talking about."

"The angelic figure called my name again. It said, "Bobby D." I asked, "Who are you and what you want?" As clear as I am hearing you speak, I heard it say, "A work to do: from the time it takes to conceive until the time it takes to give birth: 9 months." Then it went away. I got up and got a glass of water."

Houston was quiet. I know he is thinking. I sat back and waited before he said, "Bobby D. you have a work to do, and you only have nine months to do it. I take it the nine months started the beginning of July; since it came to you the beginning of June."

When he said a work to do, I gave him a cold glare. He knew what I was feeling as he stated,

"I know you been hearing about a calling on your life since you were knee high to a kitten but if you look at it, your mother maybe right about it after all."

"Yeah, but I don't think that is it" I stated dryly.

"I know you don't want to hear that, but you had a visitation."

"And?"

"Aren't you at least concerned what the work is?"

"No. My mother ruined any ideology of the "Call" for me. I don't want to be a hypocrite as she is. I would rather leave the "Call" to others that wants it; but not me."

"Aren't you a little bit puzzled as to why this is happening?"
I got up and stated, "I guess it is because I am the child of a preacher."

I walked out, and Houston did not to stop me. I closed the door and Inga asked, "You all ok in there?"

"Yeah, we good."

"You going to the small ceremony today for Mother Clark?"

"If I don't, I would have Hell on my hands with my mother if I don't show my face."

"I'm going for a few minutes then I am leaving. Baker has a little league game today at three."

"Houston going?"

"It's a church event, what do you think?"

"Maybe one of us from the family can come out and support Baker?"

"Your dad said he may come if he comes back in time."

"Where did he go?"

"I don't know. He was angry because of what I told him and that was when you arrived."

"Sure did."

"Ok. Let me get back in here and finish the statements for last month."

She walked off. Before I could leave, she asked, "Bobby D. can I talk to you for a minute?"

"Sure."

I went behind her in her office. She closed the door and said, "Someone is stealing money from this business and it's not me. I have gone over and over and over these books and still can't find out. Everything I wrote is documented but the money on the book does not match the money in the bank."

"Houston has asked me to check things out and I have been over your books."

"You have?"

"Yes, and you are right. You are initialing everywhere you are supposed to but somehow the money vanishes into thin air and that is not normal. Things on your end are lined up, but something is happening. I just don't know what, but I will find out."

"Thank you for believing me."

"It's not that I believe you, I am just glad you are being honest."

I got up and left Inga in her office.

Chapter 10

I went back to the morgue to think. I shook my head and a knock was heard. I looked up and saw my dad. He came in and said, "What you doing back here?"

"Nothing. I just walked back here. I was upfront. Where you been?"

"Running errands."

"You going to the small ceremony this afternoon for Mother Clark?"

"If I don't, I would have to fight your mother."

We laughed as I said, "Inga was telling me about Baker's game today."

"That's right. I am going to go to the ceremony for a little bit. I guess I will leave after your mother gets up and say a few words."

"I might do the same. I really don't care to go."

"I know you don't but do it out of respect."

"That may be the only reason why I will go and be seen. But dad, I really don't care what they think about me. I know they think I'm weird because I don't socialize with them."

"Bobby, you never have socialized with them, and you probably never will. The people at the church are people your mother deals with."

"I know even after being gone for eight years, they still haven't changed."

"What you think about the funeral home business so far?"

"I don't think anything. I will help this place be better so I can go back in hiding."

"You wouldn't want to run this place?"

"No. I love working with the dead, but I don't want this place. This isn't my life; it's yours but Houston for sure."

"I'm glad you said that."

"Said what?"

"Said how you don't want this place."

"Well, I don't."

"Today I willed it over to Houston and if he dies before me, it will be sold to the highest bidder; with the money going to his sons or whoever has custody of them. Either way I am walking away from the business. I am getting old, and I need to start relaxing."

"Dad. That's great. Are you going to tell him?" I said with excitement.

"I am but I wanted to run it by you first. You are my only child, and I didn't want you to think I didn't want you to have this place."

"You made a great decision because I don't want this place. I have my own money, and I placed the boys in my will to have it all, if I don't have children."

"You want children Bobby D.?"

"After being raised by you but mainly my mom, no. I won't have the heart to force religion or callings upon a child while I live like Satan himself. I would wait until the Lord delivers me from things like my own mind."

"You know your mother's action, even mine is our own accountability. We can't make people go to heaven just because they may have lived a sanctified life. They should make it there themselves. The Word is right all by itself and it's up to every individual to find their way. A preacher can tell you how you should do but it's up to you to do it."

"I have a lot of resentment in me. I can't stand when people claim to be one thing then I find out they are the complete opposite. Just the other day, Inga was telling me about her friend and that married man."

"Yeah, I heard about that."

"I don't like it when people do stuff like that then expects the person that was hurt not to be hurt. How is that? They both played a portion in hurting that wife, but her friend was upset because her child's life was lost. Sins of the parent's fall to the children. Parents need to read their bible and apply it to how they are living and then someone can feel sorry when things happen. Like what Moses said, "How he would rather suffer with God and do right than to suffer without God by doing wrong." People want to do wrong and want the blessing of God on their lives. They need to wake up because if we don't change our ways, our way of living will show us up and we won't like it."

My dad was listening. It was like I had put something on his mind. I was quiet before I stated further, "I guess I have a whole lot of bitter to uproot. I hate the fact I've always felt forced to live a called life after witnessing how messed up my mom's life was."

"Ask for forgiveness and let Jesus do it."

To change the subject I asked, "Do you really love my mom? I mean I just want to know. I never felt you didn't but I don't know. I'm grown and so are you. I think that is why I am asking because I don't believe you do."

He sat down and said, "I will be honest. She is a wonderful woman in her own right; she is thoughtful and does what she thinks is right to keep the family together. I don't like her hypocritical lifestyle but all in all, I love her but I am not in love with her."

When my dad Lee spoke that statement, he looked as if a weight had been lifted off him. I don't know why but he seemed lighter when he confessed that. I am not judging and I know he has been faithful to her unlike her to him. I was getting angry because for some reason I believe my dad is about to tell me a lie. I had to ask softly, "Does she know this? Does she know she is doing all she can for a man that does not love her like he should?"

"Yes and no. We don't have a whole lot of secrets from each other but those are things she and I could work on and out. We are together to keep face and, in a way, we want the love back but it is not working. She has been worldlier than anything. First it was the drinking and the cursing. Now she's smoking those stinking cigarettes and still drinking. It has been hard for me and us. Then you left and made it harder for me. I tried finding you but you covered your tracks very well."

I gave a small laugh. My dad said, "It does not mean that we don't love you."

"I know. It just means you both love each other less."

He sounded as if he was trying to convince me by stating, "I'm trying to make it up to you by being a better person to Baker and Houston Lee."

"Well do what you think you must. We can't go back in the past and rewrite it."

"Thanks. Bobby."

"We better get cleaned up and get headed out to the church to show our faces" I spoke so he would leave.

We both laughed as we got up. He asked with laughter, "You riding with me or you going in that vehicle of yours; which, causes people to stare?"

"I'm taking the hearse. I like the way people wonder what is going on."

My dad gave me a hug as he laughed on out the room. The door closed behind him and now I am alone with my thoughts. *How long have they been living a lie for my sake? I should have asked him but I don't think he would have been completely honest with me because that meant him telling me how it's been all my life. That also meant him having to admit he knows of her secrets about Houston, and I know he wouldn't dare tell that. What I don't get is how did I miss the signs? I saw behind the scenes how lovely they acted and how they kept thrusting God in my face. Honestly, I never saw them being loving at all.*

My dad was always quiet. I guess that is why they hid it so well. She probably let him do what he wanted if he was discrete. I kept pondering *how could, I not have seen his answers coming? I wanted to ask him about Houston because he has already changed his will. I started to say I wanted it but I don't like lying. I should have just to see him squirm and get out of whatever it is he is trying to do.*

Once again, I shut my thoughts off and went inside to change clothes. However, I was not prepared as I walked inside. There sitting perched on the couch arm was my mother. Her in her old age, was acting like she was about to fly like a bird. I eased up on her and she howled at me like an owl. My mother called out, "Stay back. I saw a snake in the house. I have to sit up here so when I see it I can catch it."

"Where you see it at?"

"I saw it over there. It's long and gray" she pointed at the broom in the kitchen.

To patronize her, I ran over to the broom and jumped on it like I was really wrestling with a huge snake. She was making sounds as I choke and threw the broom. I picked it up from top to bottom and threw it outside. Quickly I slammed the door. She got down off the couch edge and stood up to say, "Thank you but I could have gotten it."

"I know but we don't have too much time. Mother Clark's ceremony is in another hour and I know you didn't need to get all sweaty from wrestling that big snake."

She kind of looked sadden at the mention of her friend's name. I stated, "Are you up to going?"

"Yes. I am speaking and I wouldn't miss it for the world."

I looked her up and down. Her eyes had a wide look of someone who hadn't slept in days. Her clothes were not as neat usual and I'm sure no one would pay it any mind because of who she is in the church. I know she is in no condition to drive and I really didn't care but to watch my own back I asked, "You want to ride with me?"

"Are you going in that hearse you been driving since you got here?"

"What else am I going to ride in?"

"We can go in my BMW."

"Only if I drive."

"That will be fine. Oh wait. Is your dad going with us?"
I decided to use this time to see what she knows. I stated, "He may come. You know Baker has a game today and it starts at two."

Mother kind of hump her shoulders and responded in a snappy way, "He might go to it."

"Why you say it like that? Someone has to show support to the little guy."

"That's what his momma and daddy are for."

"But how can they if they are always doing things for the church or doing whatever you need them to do?"

"That's not my concern. They have to figure that out on their own; I did."

She does know something, I thought as I got ready. We got in her car my mother sat on the other side not speaking. Suddenly she yelled out, "Don't hit the old man in the road!"

I looked and it was a poster of a gorilla eating bananas. I laughed inwardly and replied, "I won't hit him. He's eating."

Out of breath and holding her chest mother commented, "I didn't think you saw him or that baby in his mouth."

This will be interesting I thought as I parked in her parking spot. People were a little interested as to why I was driving my mother; since I seldom come to the services. She got out and greeted the people. I kind of walked behind her because I didn't know what to expect. She walked inside and greeted people. I nodded and kept it moving. I made sure I didn't hold conversation with anyone because these people are nosey.

I went in the sanctuary and sat in the back. Mother sat in her seat as people came in. Teona had the urn decorated on the table in a lovely fashion.

The pianist began playing as a woman started singing. The song was sad but I didn't feel any sorrow for Mother Clark. I watched and listened as people made Mother Clark sound like a saint. They went on and on about her and her generosity. It was boring me. My dad was there and I nodded for him to come outside. He held his finger up and went outside. I went around the corner where he was and said, "Something was wrong with mom?"

"What you mean? She looks perfectly fine."

"When I got home she was on the couch saying a big snake was in the kitchen. She was pointing at the broom. I wrestled with it as I threw it outside."

"That is strange."

"I know."

"How she get here?"

"I drove us in her car."

"That's thoughtful of you Bobby."

"I thought I'll let you know before anything else jumps off."
"What you mean anything else?"

"On the way, she told me not to hit the old man. It turns out the old man was a gorilla on a poster board eating bananas."

Dad was somewhat silent before he asked, "You reckon the loss of her friend is doing something to her or maybe it is something else?"

"I don't know but I had to tell you before you left for Baker's game."

"Yeah. I am about to leave now. I've showed my face and now I can go. You going to stay home tonight."

"Where else am I going to stay?"

"Lately I think you been at the funeral home more than you be in the house with us."

"I do. I find more rest and comfort among the dead."

He didn't comment as he walked off. I went back in the church as he left for the game. Houston saw me. He had tears in his eyes as he held my mother in his arms. I wonder what happened while I was outside with my dad. The people were bidding farewell to the urn as they hugged Teona. I didn't want to look like the bad guy so I didn't go to it all. If I had of, I would have wanted to knock it off and sweep the ashes in the trash for pick on Monday morning.

I already told Teona I was sorry and I was not saying it again. People need to know when enough is enough and these people here don't have a clue. They all are still on their way to Hell like they were all those years before I left. Houston walked mother over to me as she was crying. I murmured, "Why she crying so hard?"

"I don't know. She just started crying and has not been able to stop" he whispered.

"Let me take her on home so she can rest" I whispered back.

"Yeah, go on and do that. I might call and check on her after a while. You going to be there?" he lipped.

"Yeah, my dad is going to Baker's game" I lip back.

"I know. Teona has asked me to come by for the small repast she is having at Mother Clark's home" he whispered.

We put my mom in the car and closed the door. I spoke, "I was getting tired of all that whispering and lipping."

"Me too" Houston spoke with humor.

"Is that ok with Tina? I mean who gets what?"

"I don't know but I will be there for comfort for any that needs it."

"I can bring the hearse and shake things up a bit" I said in comedy.

Houston laughed as he said, "Just take your mom home and make sure she rest."

I took mom home and she was soundless the entire trip. Being guilty for lacing her cigarettes never bothered me. Smoking kills and it will eventually kill her; why not let her see how it feels to play with the life of someone who wanted nothing but to be left alone. I looked over at her and she was sound asleep. When we made it home, I helped her inside and put her to bed. Once she was in her room, I decided to do something different. I watched TV.

September
Chapter 11

The next few weeks went by so fast. Before I knew it, September was here and so was the cool weather. Mother had been herself off and on but I won't worry about that. I told her the cigarettes were bad and making her a little looney, but she didn't believe me. From time to time, she would smoke them and when she did her behavior would be altered. Sometimes I didn't know if she was going or coming but it mattered not.

I was embalming more and more people, and the business was looking good but when I checked the financial status it didn't show that. The status really showed a decline and how money was still coming up missing. I checked behind Inga and she was telling the truth. Somewhere somehow, the records indicated someone was tampering with the books and it was making Inga and Houston look guilty.

Personally, I know they are not stealing because I have been watching their spending and their assets. They had nothing to show for the money that is being taken from the business. They weren't in a financial strain so stealing to keep up a lavish lifestyle was not the problem. In fact, they weren't broke, but they barely made ends meet.

There had been times, when I helped them out anonymously because I know Houston would not take it otherwise.

Inga didn't shop or overspend on anything. She clipped coupons and maps out her route daily to avoid back tracking and saving gas. Now here is the kicker. My dad had changed. He has started coming home later and later. He would mostly come home while mom and I was asleep but I don't be. I am always up and waiting on the time he comes home and listening earnestly for his behavior and timing him.

In the morning time, he would be the first one up and the first one gone. During the day, my mother would do missionary work at the hospice homes, convalescent homes and jails on Tuesdays. Half the time, she doesn't even know where my dad is. When he said they only do things keep up appearances he did not lie. Now I see what he was telling me but being a young child, you would think your parents are too busy for you but the truth is they stay busy to stay away from each other.

I went to the funeral home and to tell Houston what I think. I know I am going to need a whole lot of evidence to back it up. If I don't he won't believe me. I made it to the funeral home and no one was there. I got out and went through the back door. I turned the alarm off and went inside. No one was up front and I thought it to be strange. It is almost eight thirty and no one is around but me. Seconds later, Houston knocked on the door and I unlocked it for him as I said, "Good morning."

"Good morning. You been here long?"

"No, I just got in. Where's Inga?"

"She's coming. She had a few errands to run and drop the boys off at day care."

"Good we need to talk."

"Come on in my office."

"How is your mom doing?"

"Ok, I guess."

"You guess?" he asked as he looked back at me.

"I guess. I don't see her much and I don't talk to her much."

"Oh. Ok" he spoke as I followed behind him to his office. He opened the door and turned the light on. I closed the door before I sat down. He was putting his brief case down as he asked, "What's on your mind?"

"I think my dad is the one stealing from the business."

Houston stopped and looked at me strangely. Slowly he sat down and stared at me. His first words were, "You better have proof to back it up because you are accusing the man I looked up to as my dad of stealing."

"I know it sounds crazy."

"You darn right it does. He just told me that he is giving me the business and now you come along and tell me he is stealing from the business he just willed."

"How do you think I feel knowing my dad is stealing from the business I am to help save? I know it doesn't sound nor look right. I went over my findings a thousand times and each time everything pointed to him."

"How is that?"

"Let me start with you."

"What about me?"

"You barely keep your head above the water. You have a high mortgage, student loans and if you weren't receiving private funding, you would be drowning in debt right now. You don't have time to get near the money, and you don't have a strong enough communication with your wife to tell her to swindle the money for you."

"The private funding; it's you isn't it?"

Pretending to not know what he was getting at, I asked him "Me what?"

"It's you Bobby D. You were the one paying our bills and doing all the other stuff for me and my family."

I stared at him before saying, "Yes, it's me. I did it because I knew you wouldn't accept it any other way. I have plenty of money and I don't mind giving it to the one person I would trust with my life. You have been family when I didn't feel like I had a family. You are more than mere cousin blood you are blood. So why not help you when I see you are doing your best with what you have."

"Thank you, Bobby D. You don't know how much that means to me. I can pay you back soon as I can."

"That was why I was doing it without you knowing. I don't want you to pay me back. I don't want nor need, your money. I did it because I wanted too with nothing in return."

"What can I do to show my gratitude?"

"Do what is best for you and the family" I said with a smile.

He got up and gave me a hug. I hugged him back as he sat back down in his chair. I hated I told him, but he already knew in a way. I just confirmed what he thought. We were nonverbal before Houston started speaking, "I don't make a whole lot of money here. I used to but since the money been coming up missing, I took a pay cut to make up for the difference. I have always loved working here and I would do all I can to make sure the business lives, but I can't stand a thief. I know it means my family would not have much, but I am looking at the big picture. I know the business isn't going to stay down forever and when it turns around I would get the money. So far it hadn't happened and the money is missing left and right and I can't catch it. You say you think your dad is getting it but I don't believe it without hard core evidence. I believe my wife is stealing the money. It has to be her."

I shook my head no as I replied, "She's not. Your wife's not stealing the money."

"What makes you so sure she isn't the thief? All the money goes through her hands. No one else has access to the funds but my wife. Some of the time I think she doesn't want me with my own boys."

"Why you say that? They are yours."

"I try spending time with them, and she makes up excuses as to why I don't need to do this or that. I got to the point where I just don't try. I spend all my time trying to make sure that other people's families are happy when they lose their love one."

"That doesn't make sense, but Inga is not stealing from the business. She doesn't have any habits that require money. There aren't any hidden accounts, and her personal account might have fifty dollars in it. She takes the money she makes here to help pay your family expenses and she is on a budget. Inga even maps out her trips to do everything to save gas. Neither one of you has assets nor anything of a value, might I add. Your wife doesn't shop and she clips coupons. Inga doesn't have a whole lot of time to do anything, but I did notice one thing. She is hiding something small."

"Hiding something small" Houston asked me as if he knew something he wasn't going to tell me.

"You two are arguing and making your children's lives miserable. Lately you both have been distant, and you both blame the other's way of living. You don't spend time together. The truth is you spend all your time with church members, and you leave her alone too much. She is always with the children and has no life of her own. Everywhere and everything she does consist of the boys while you have it made."

"I don't have it made."

"You don't share any of the parenting of the boys. You leave everything up to her but you want to show her off. You tell people how you all are doing so well but if it weren't for Inga busting her butt and doing what needs to be done, you would have been broke long before now."

"How do you know that?"

"It's my job to know everything and when I say everything, I mean everything."

"But your dad; stealing? I can't grasp that."

"Yes, I am working on that as we speak."

"I think my wife has something to do with it She just has too."

"Why is it easier to believe your wife is guilty and my dad is innocent? It looks like you should have Inga's back, but you don't. I don't get that Houston."

"I think my wife is hiding something and I don't know what. She is suspect to me and I been praying for the Lord to reveal it to me. I've asked for the spirit of truth to be in our home."

"Has she been telling the truth?"

"My gut says so but her actions don't line up."

"You know she is telling the truth you just hope she isn't."

"That could be it but I know the money is coming up missing."

"Do you remember when Mother Clark was alive, and you sent me over to her house?"

"What about it?"

"She did say a few things."
He sat up and asked, "What did she say to you?"

"She told me she believes someone is stealing from the business. She opened the envelope and took a look at the check. She looked at me and spoke how it didn't look like her writing and how she swears every month Inga doesn't know what she is doing because every time she looked around her checks are lost or she is told how she didn't sign it. She said she may be old but she knows they are stealing. She says she spends good money every week and yet you all act like the church and the business is broke. I thought she was just being old but when I checked out the finances the first time without telling you I knew the old bat was onto something."

Houston sat back in his chair and asked, "Have you spoken any of this to your dad or Inga?"

"As for Inga, we spoke and she swears she isn't stealing. As for my dad, not as much about anything. I don't want to spook him off, in case he is the one doing the stealing."

"Think about it Bobby D. He has signed it over to me so why would he keep stealing if it is him? The findings you are telling me don't add up."

"I don't know but I think all of this is a set up for something greater."

"You might be right."

I got up and said, "Don't mention it to any of them. Let's pretend it's over. I want to see what the next move will be for any of them."

"I won't."

I left out his office and went straight to mine. When I got to my office, I did my monthly inventory and this time, it was more than usual. Seconds later Inga rushed in my sanctuary and yelled out, "You got to get home. Your mother is on top of the house claiming she can fly!"

I did not question her. I rushed out the back door and jumped in the hearse. I wasn't driving too fast but when I got there the police and the ambulance people were there. Being who I am, I made my way through the small crowd. The police tried stopping me, but I told them I was her child, and they let me through.

When I saw the great and powerful Gloria Reed, she had two feathers that came off the mural in her living room. She had one in each hand. She was flapping and flapping. By the time she saw me she yelled out, "Bobby you come to watch me fly?"

I started to tell her, "Do a somersault or a nose dive" but they were all looking and doing all they can to talk her down. I replied instead, "I want you to come down so we can talk."

"You want me to fly down to you?"

This was very funny. I wish I could record this, but time is at hand and too many witnesses. Here I am trying to talk down the mighty Gloria Reed. She took my life through Hell all because she didn't know when enough was enough. She made me angry and bitter. But she is the one on top of house, with the threat of jumping. I saw I was taking too long as I said, "Let me come up to you."

"You got wings too?"

"Yeah. Let me come up and show you."

"Come on. I'm ready to feel the wind beneath me."

You will feel the ground too, I thought as I went to the shed and got a ladder. The men held it stable as I climbed on top of the house. She turned back and saw me. My hallucinating mother had a puzzle on her face as she questioned, "Where are your wings, Bobby? Are you not going to fly with me?"

I loved it as I stammered loud enough for her to hear me, "I think you are to do the church world a favor and jump to your dejected death."

"You think that would help you too?"

"It would but others would miss you."

"They will?"

"Sure, they will. You are the wonderful influential leader, Gloria Reed. Everyone loves you and you can do no wrong. All you have to do is speak and you have whatever it is you ask. It doesn't matter if people are on their way to Hell because you tell them one thing and they are too stupid to listen to God for themselves. Relax and close your eyes" I said as she allowed me to walk up on her.

I was almost to her as I stated, "Can't you hear the birds singing?"

"Oh, yes I can."

"Can't you feel the cool wind's breeze upon your skin?"

"This breeze is nice Bobby."

"That's right keep your eyes close and let me catch you."

That sentence was the last she heard as I snatched her backwards. We almost tumbled off the house, but I kept it from happening. Luckily, she is not fat or we both would have been maggot food. Let me take that back. She would have been maggot food because I was going to make sure I fell on top of her.

She didn't know what was happening as the policemen met me at the top of the ladder to get her. My dad was already in the ambulance waiting for them to take her to the hospital for evaluation. She was crying as I called out, "Mom I will be right behind you."

My dad seems sincere and terrified because he could have lost his wife today. I got in the hearse and drove behind them. Once we got to the hospital they took her to the seventh floor. The psychiatrists were there, and they had me to fill out some information on her. My dad was at a loss for words because this was unlike her and I felt the same way; to a degree.

I made sure to mention she just lost her closest and dearest friend through a sudden death. This loss could be the cause of this trauma she is facing. They all agreed but will do further testing of her. Houston showed up and I told him what occurred. He was surprised as well. My dad was holding on to the best of his ability. I knew he was doing all he could to be strong but Houston and I both know how sentimental my dad can be.

I also made a mention that the church should allow her to step down until further notice. I also stated Houston should be the senior pastor until she comes back around. He said the church board would have to vote on it. I told him to get with them and assure them he is not taking her place; he only wants to fill it until she does better. I sat back like a fat cat eating cheese as I watched them all being played. However, Houston and my dad both agreed on my suggestion; like I knew they both would.

October
Chapter 12

My mom stayed on the seventh floor for the rest of September and almost all of October. Today is the last week of October and she gets to come home as people get in the Halloween spirit. The church is having a welcome home party at the church for her and I have to attend. Dad had gone to get her as I am sitting here in her study. My mind recalled my younger years as I was in there talking to her and it were right before I left.

I looked around her study and knew I wasn't going to be here long. I have two teenage boys to embalm from a hunting accident. Doing them is more important than being here around these fake people. I thought, *I must admit, since she hasn't been smoking the secret dipped smokes, she should be back to her old self again. I don't know if she has given up smoking, but I will make sure she sees them. I even wondered why I going through all the trouble to bring her down or to the brink of destruction. The answer is easy she pushed me away from her and God. Nothing I did coming up as a child was good enough because I did not care to preach as she does.*

The truth is I cared to preach. I just didn't care to trick and mislead the people like she did.

Because of the way she pushed me, I enable myself to be in a position to push back. Now I am pushing back, I will show her who pushes the hardest. I've reached the breaking point in my life whenever I am told that I have a work to do for the Lord. It's not that I don't believe it, I just want to find it on my own, in my own way.

Words can't describe the way I felt growing up and watching her tear down my life.
I would have been happier if she just left me alone, but she didn't. My mother started including me in her secrets and before you know it I am in her schemes to dilute the Word to the people. I didn't want to do that. Sad enough, I've found myself bitter, angry and resenting everything she stands for when it comes to God.

I don't care to go to church, and I don't care to be helped. I just want to be left alone but I know I can't stay in this shape. I know I need the Lord, but I don't believe I can allow my heart to feel. The military has built on my foundation of lack of emotions. In a way, I have buried myself in hopes that one can find me. Maybe something is wrong with me? I can see myself taking a pair of pliers and skinning my mother alive. With each rip of her skin, I would talk to her by telling her of the way she did me.

And when she became unresponsive, I would take those same pliers and pull out her teeth one by one until she is bleeding and toothless. If that wasn't enough, I would take a fork and stretch her brown eyes so far out her head; that the nerve string is still attached. That string would give her head so much pain as I use a lighter to scan the nerve, up and down until she hollers out. The way I want to torture her does not compare to the pain she has given me.

A knock was heard and it was Houston. He came in and said, "Your mother is out front and she is happy. I think her being gone has helped her a lot. What you think?"

"I think any help is an improvement."

"That's right but your mom seems so alive and well. You gonna come out to see her?"

"Yeah, I'll come for a few" I said as I turned my head.

Houston came in the study and asked, "What you thinking about? You seem so far away."

"I was lost in my childhood but other than that, it's Halloween and I am thinking how I can scare some people tonight."

"Bobby D. scare some people?" Houston laughed as he said that to me.

"Why not?"

"I know you've scared Baker and since that incident in the embalming room, he won't go near the funeral home."

I laughed as I proclaimed, "He should have listened when I told him to get out."

"I believe he has learned his lesson. When I tell him to do something he does it and he prays every night and day. He says he's not going to die without God living in him."

"He's right as long as you both don't push him into something he may not be ready for or keep telling him about a call on his life because you have a call on yours."

"I don't plan to do to my sons what your parents did to you. I know they meant well but somewhere along the way they damaged you. I don't know to what extreme, but I know you are harboring some painful feelings towards your mom; since she did the most damage."

"You right. She did and I am feeling crazy on the inside about her. I have tried to stop feeling this way, but the truth is I haven't tried hard enough. I speculate feeling like this is a safety net for me. I don't want to get hurt by her or my dad's lack of parenting. Go on and say how you think I am crazy for feeling like this after all these years."

"You are not crazy. I grew up in the house with you but I don't see it the way you do."

"Why would you? You were the child they longed to have. You can convince or motivate people to see things your way; just like her. You took on the Word of God and ran with it when they told you about a calling on your life?"

"That's because I took a hold to it. You didn't grow up being blamed for your mother dying. I did. I could have easily rejected any calling or whatever you want to call it on my life but I didn't. I wanted it. I wanted to serve God with a meaningful purpose and to live for HIM was the only way I could do that. Sure, your parents weren't hard on me because I accepted what they told me or maybe they weren't hard on me because they felt sorry for me. You on the other hand will not let anyone tell you something until you believe it yourself. Bobby D. you have always been like that. Your parents could not understand that because you are their only child and by that they pushed and pushed, until you could not take it anymore. I've studied how that type of push your parents gave you could cause one to become evil and possibly a killer. I don't see that in you. I see an individual that rebelled against parents that didn't understand their child. I see an individual that has allowed the past to control their future. You got a warning from the visitation. I think you need to take heed."

I just watched him be all in his feelings as I stated, "Soon as I can, I have to get back to business. I have bodies to prepare because the funerals were moved up."

As if he forgot he called out with a loud tone, "We do have one of those young boy's funerals to do this Friday and the other one on Saturday."

"We do and I'll have them done on time and looking just as good dead as they did alive."

He stood up and began to walk off as he said, "Bobby D. I have no doubt. You always do your best."

"Wait. You going to have treats when I come by?"

He stopped and said when he turned around, "Yeah for the young kids."

"I guess you get a trick."

"Sorry not into that. Inga is going out with a few friends tonight while I have the boys. We don't do that costume thing and every year I explain the true meaning behind "Holy Ween." I am taking them, well Baker to the movies then out to eat. If you going to do all that running around town, how you going to have time to do the bodies tonight?"

"I am working late. What else do I have to do? No one will be there but me so why not go slow and perfect my art."

"I'll see you later Bobby D."

He gave me a smile and closed the door. I got and followed outside. The people were all hovering over mother as if she was Mary of the bible. I spoke to a few people and gave my mom a hug. She looks the same but with a little more weight. My dad was being the loyal caring husband I have always known him to be as he talked with ease. I saw Inga with a few ladies from the church as they were all making plans.

No doubt to go to a costume party of some sort; for that is a big deal in this town. I usually don't participate but tonight I will. I have a few people I want to go visit. Before I could leave out, my dad stopped me. I didn't want to talk because I have a long night ahead of me. He asked, "What's the rush?"

"I am going out tonight in costume."

"You? Going to dress up. In costume? On Halloween? When you start participating in that?"

"I normally don't do it but for some reason I want to have some fun. For some reason, I want to do it."

"Then what else you have planned?"

"Go home and go to bed because tomorrow I have those two bodies for the upcoming funerals, remember."

"Sure do. I was going to go out for a few with the Deacons."

"Go head. You need a break like everyone else."

"I don't want to leave your mother alone. Tonight's her first night back home."
I glanced over at mother and looked back at him to say, "She will be fine. Those old hags, I mean the ladies will be happy to keep Mother alert. I should be there when the news goes off if not before then. Go on out and enjoy yourself. You have been by her side every day and not just because of this incident. You have always been by her side. I have not ever seen otherwise. I'm sure she will understand."

"Ok. Go on out and scare some people" my dad said with a hearty laugh.
I gave him a hug and left. When I got in the car, I forgot to tell him I would probably end my night early and go on and do the embalming like I told Houston. *He'll be alright,* I thought as I drove to the funeral home. When I made it to the funeral home, I parked my hearse and cleaned it up. I decided on adding a casket for a great touch. I drove to the house and got in my costume.

My parents were still at the church. I didn't know what I would be. Then it hit me. I would be a tall figurine. I would be the one that came to see me. I put on the all black robe with my white gloves. I placed black makeup on my face and put a regular stick in my hand. I looked almost like what I saw. Even I scared myself some. I got in the hearse and made my way to the retirement communities. When I pulled up children were coming from all over from different houses.

I parked the hearse at the office, which is located right outside the gate. I got my stick and began walking. The children kept looking at me and some of the parents walked opposite of me. For the entirety of my walk all eyes were on me. The first house I stopped at had children waiting for the old woman to bring the bowl of goodies. I walked far enough for her to see me. The children had their backs turned to me but when she saw me, she dropped the bowl. Her face went as white as snow, but the children paid me no attention. I walked a little further and pointed at the defenseless old woman. She trembled as she stumbled backwards. I walked off and skipped a few houses. I went to the next house. It was an older black woman and man. They opened the door and there I stood. They did not panic but the man asked, "You come to get me?"

He was so sincere. I shook my head no and pointed at his wife. She called on the name of Jesus as I walked off into the night. I drove to another community. I mostly walked around without saying a word. The parents of the children were looking at me up and down as I walked up and down the streets. I even skipped a few houses. Many of the children were afraid of me and many of the parents were too. It was funny how the parents would snatch the child up as I walked near. Some of the children would cry because they recognized who I am or what I represent. Every Christian or claim to be Christian knows what the grim reaper or the angel of death looks like. I guess I choose it because I work with death and dying is a natural part of life; like living.

While I was walking in this community, I came across a child. She was cross dressed between a ballerina and an angel with flawless makeup to be as young as she is. I nodded to her, and she said, "I am a ballerina angel princess."

I nodded my head in approval. She said, "You are the angel that takes people down there, aren't you?"

I nodded again. She said, "Well you not gone take me because I been good and I believe in God."

"What's HIS name?" I asked hoarsely.

"HIS name is Jesus, but we call HIM God."

I nodded and she said, "You don't need to be with dead people. You need to be with live people. You need to be in a place where there is a heaven and just because we are raised one way it doesn't mean we have to be that way. My parents love me but they know I make a choice to do right. They raised me good."

The child's mother called for her. She said, "I have to go. I hope you decide that you want to be an angel for the Lord and not the devil angel."

She ran off in the direction of her mother. I was puzzled. I went back to the hearse and took the hood off. I cried. For the first time in my life, I was crying, and I was feeling remorseful for the wrong I have done. Maybe I had it all wrong and was fooled into thinking my parents were the bad guys because of the way they brought me up. I can't believe I could have killed my mother.

Although, I didn't like the way she had done me as a child, it gave me no right to purposely endanger her life like I did. I have been tricked. And when I think about my dad and how he kept being faithful to my overbearing, persuasive, conniving preacher mother I felt bad. How could I have told my own dad I thought he was weak? He told me he knew my mother was wrong, but he can't raise her. I understood but here I am having evil feelings inside of me that need to be done away with.

I don't know how I made my way to the funeral home, but I was sitting outside in the hearse crying and crying. I must get my act together. I closed my eyes and lifted my hands. In a humble tone I said, *"Lord forgive me of my sins; mainly the known. I have blamed my parents for making me vindictively angry towards them and you when they were doing what they felt was right. Help me to be a better child to you and them. Amen."*

When I prayed sense of peace swept over me. It was like I was happy and actually thankful for being who I am. I've decided to be a better child to my parents and maybe just maybe discover for myself what my calling is. I dried my eyes and got out the hearse. I am going to embalm both of these young boys and go home so I can ask for forgiveness from my parents. I unlocked the back door, and the alarm didn't go off. *That's odd,* I thought as I set it and locked the door back.

I walked up the hall to the embalming room when I heard a sound. I realized I didn't turn the light on. *What if it's an intruder?* I thought as I tiptoed lightly to the end of the hallway. I saw nothing out of the ordinary. I looked around and even went to the front glass doors. They were locked and I shrugged it off. Before I could make it back to the hall, I heard it again. It sounded like a soft moan coming from the room I use when I am here.

My heart was beating and thumping like a drummer in a band. I didn't know what to expect. Taking my time, I walked up to the door and put my ear to it. From the other side, of the door slow music was playing and grunts; more like a man's moaning could be heard. I thought back and didn't see any cars outside. My dad is out with the deacons, Houston has the boys, Inga is out with her friends, my mom is at home, and I am here. Anyone with ties to this business is accounted for.

Now I'm thinking someone has broken in and being creative. *Probably some dare devil couple* I thought as I listened for voices. All I could hear was moaning and body sticking more likely from moisture. I took my time and turned the doorknob slowly. The door eased open without making a sound. From the small glitch, I saw clothes on the floor and a lot of candles to brighten the room. It was romantic for flower petals were everywhere.

Further up my eyes went, I saw my dad. He was on his back with his chest exposed. He was not alone. I could not tell who the woman was on top of him was at first. She had her hair hanging down her braless back and she appeared to have an ivory skin tone. Just by looking at her from the waist up, she

195

appeared to be medium built. I didn't know her until she said, "Is it good to you Lee?"

My ears became frozen and numb as my mouth flew open. I could not gander at the sight anymore; for I just saw Inga making love to my dad. Before I could slowly walk backwards my dad looked right into my face through the small crack. He threw her off him and she called out, "What's wrong Lee?"

I was walking quietly and very fast as he yelled to her, "I thought I heard something. Let me go check it out."

I could not believe I just saw my dad and Inga. I must be mistaken but I know I wasn't as I trotted down the hall with the view still playing in my head. Quickly behind me was my dad. He had a sheet around him as he called after me above a whisper, "Bobby. Bobby D."

I kept going. He reached me as I made it to the back door. He said with sweat all over him, "Let me explain."

I could only shake my head no as I took out. He stood there and hit the wall as I got in my hearse and left. I could not accept what I saw as true. I just talked to the Lord about being better to my parents and how my dad has always been faithful and now this. How could he sleep with his nephew's wife? How could she cheat on Houston with his uncle? So many questions came to me, and I didn't want to know the answers.

My mother and Houston are the victims in this affair they are committing. I never thought I would be siding with my mother after all she did me the most damage. But my dad? He was always by her side and always the one who in my eyes was the innocent one. I see now he had me fooled. My mind thought of Houston and the boys. Something like this could damage his family home as well as shake his faith.
I arrived at home and just sat there. I didn't go in. I didn't want to see my mother. I didn't want to look in her face and call on the name of Jesus for all I done wrong and what I just witnessed. I don't know what to do but I do know that I am hurt.

November
Chapter 13

I woke up on the first day of November to the sound of light tapping on the window. It was my dad. I rolled my eyes as I turned my head. He said, "Bobby D. get out the car and please talk to me. You have to hear me out."
He backed up so I could get out the car. I turned up my nose in disgust when my words replied, "We don't have anything to talk about."

I got out and walked off from him. He called out silently, "They don't know."
I stopped for a few seconds, and I walked into the house. I have to change. I have two bodies that need embalming and finishing that should have done it last night. I went in the house. My mother was sitting at the table. She asked, "You want some breakfast before you rush off to be with the dead?"

"Naw. I will get something on my way after I get cleaned up or after I finish working."

"That's you."

Ignoring her I went in my open area and washed off. I got dressed and went back to the kitchen. My dad was there being the model husband as he was eating breakfast with my mother. I just stared at them. They each have me in on their secret. I don't like it. I really didn't like it when my mom did it but now my dad has forced my hand too. The way they are sitting together and acting, made me ill to know I belong to this sick family. My dad saw me and dropped his head. I walked out the door and got in my hearse. I crank up and drove off. Arriving at the funeral home was hard for me. I sat in the car in the back not knowing how I would face Houston this day. My dad told me neither my cousin Houston nor my mom knows of their infidelity. My dad has no idea I hurt people physically for what he and Inga are doing. Now that it is personal it makes hurting them harder.

I wanted to cry for I just gave myself to Christ last night and a hot second later I am witnessing two people I know, hurt two other people I know. I saw Houston at the back door. I know he is searching for me. I pulled myself together and got out the car. Houston called out to me, "You ok?"

"Some people would say good morning first."

"Yeah. Of course. Good morning."

"Good morning and why would you ask if I am ok?"

"You didn't do the bodies last night. You must have come back late."

"No, I got sidetracked but I will have them done in a few hours."

"When is the visitation for the first boy?"

"It's at two."

"It's just now eight. I will be on time."

I walked with him to the back door and went inside. I asked, "Where's your lovely wife?"

"Inga will be on. She is running a little late as usual."

"She must have had a long night last night?"

"She did. She came in about one or later."

"You didn't say a word?"

"I didn't have too. She knows and she won't do it again."

"I bet she won't."

"She won't what?" Houston asked.

"Come in late. She is married to the leading pastor at this time. She knows she can't be out all times of night. It could cause a reproach on the ministry."

"Thankfully she came in and went straight to sleep. Hanging out with the girls must have worn her out."

"Yeah, I can't really imagine that."

"Let me let you get to work."

I walked to the embalming room. I could not concentrate in the beginning as I sat down. I kept thinking *could I make Inga do to my dad what I made Senator Hawkins wife, Lisa do to Levar Fanning? Could I really make Inga bite the head of my dad's dick off and swallow it?* Before I witnessed them, my answer would have been no but now after thinking about it and realizing how I've been let down again; yes. I could make them my final project for free.

The part of me that did not care was reemerging. I sat in there and I sat there not able to focus. I finally snapped out of it and began embalming the first young man. I continued to work and work until the last young man was finished. Around twelve thirty Inga came in and said, "Houston wants to know if you are about ready and where you going for lunch?"

I didn't want to talk to her but for her to be in here with me, my dad must not have told her I caught them last night. I grinned and said, "Tell your husband my cousin I will probably dine in. I'm not hungry. How about you Inga?"

"What about me?"

"Are you hungry for food that isn't yours?"

She glared at me and smiled when she said, "You been working back here a little too long Bobby D. You need to get out more."

I laughed and so did she. Inga left and I was alone again. I sat back down and thought about all the private jobs I have done. I thought about all the ways women and men have paid for sinning against the ones they claim to love and think nothing is wrong. Each person I ever came across had an excuse for doing what they were caught doing; yet they all fail to realize that when you sin, it's contagious. Even if you do good, it's contagious. However, none of them cared to think about the pain and hurt they are inflicting on those around them.

They are going to pay, I thought as I sat and thought. I had called myself leaving this lifestyle alone and maybe this is my calling. Maybe getting Christian justice is my calling but it doesn't feel right. Then I remembered how great I felt after I prayed to Jesus and no sooner than I was feeling great, I saw them in the bed together. I got angry again and groaned loudly as I stated, "How could they do this!"

Then it came in a thought, *teach them a lesson they won't ever forget; in this life or the one to come.* Anything Christian I had learned went out the window. I don't understand a lot of things and mainly because I shut a lot of people out my life. As of right now, I don't want to hear anything about nothing. I am leaving this funeral home business in a few months and go back to doing what I love doing; making people pay for sinning.

Houston came in and said, "You finished on time as always Bobby D."

"You know I do my job easily, but I don't think of it as a job if you love what you do."

"I agree so how about if you get a paycheck?"

"A real check? For me?" I teased Houston.

"Yes, last month the money stayed the same so we can afford to pay you."

"Well give it to the boys."

He was shocked as he questioned with a surprised, "You want to give Baker and Houston Jr. your check?"

"Yeah, put it in a trust fund for them and they can't touch it until they get twenty-one."

"I don't know what to say."

"Say nothing. Just do it but if you can't do it; give it to me and I will."

"Doing it is no problem."

"Good. I have a lot of things on my mind, and I won't have the time to do it. I trust you will do it."

"I will and thank you again Bobby D."

"No. Thank your God."

He walked out then came back in to say, "I almost forgot. Where you want to eat at today?"

"I told Inga to tell you I was dining in today."

"She did but I thought you might have changed your mind."

"No. no change of mind."

We laughed as he left me alone with my thoughts. For hours at a time, I found things to stay busy. I became so in tuned with my work that I didn't know it was five o'clock. The time never bothered me because I have been known to sleep in the room up the hall but that is tainted now by them. I went home and hopefully dodge my parents; altogether.

The next few weeks brought on Thanksgiving. They all decided to have the holiday at the church. I was kind of glad because that meant I wouldn't be left alone with Inga or my parents. I had arrived a little later than my family because I like to make an appearance then disappear just as fast. Soon as I fixed me a plate and went outside, Inga came over to me. I turned my back because I didn't want to speak to her but she tapped me on the shoulder to say, "Houston told me what you did with your paycheck. I just want to say thank you."

"I did it for the children."

She was staring at me. I looked at her as if I could see right through her. Inga asked a dumbfounded question, "Are you avoiding me? Have I done something to hurt you?"

I jerked around and from behind her I saw my dad shaking his head no. I replied, "No you haven't done anything. I just been on one lately and all the things I have been dealing with, is the cause."

"Ok. I thought I would ask because you haven't been the same in a few weeks and I was just wondering."

"You did right. No excuse me. Let me see what my dad wants."

I walked off from her and walked over to him. He said, "I didn't tell her that you caught us in the room a month ago on Halloween."

I was unresponsive as he went on to say, "We need to talk but not here and not now."

"You are right and trust me when I say we will talk; WE WILL TALK but on my terms." My dad did not get a chance to say anything else. I left him standing there. I went back inside and sat near my mother. I didn't want to do that but being near her was better than being near him. At least, I know my mother can be an open snake but my dad; I never knew he was a snake until that night. Closing my thoughts off, I pretended to be the golden child my mother can praise. However, I was enjoying her and the church people a little bit better than I ever thought. I want to say it is because my mother is no longer the Pastor, and she hasn't said anything to me about my calling or a work I have to do. For the most, I am happy about it. That night when we all got home, I slept. I couldn't have been sleep long when I heard, *"Four months left."* I snatched myself upright and expected to see the messenger, but I saw nothing. I know I heard it say four months left. I back counted the months and; indeed, four months are left. I sat up on the edge of the day bed and woke on up. *Four months and then what?* I thought because I didn't know.

Things had started off good when I decided to do right but that selfsame hour, my world was twisted and broken by my dad. Sometimes it is hard for me to even think about the two of them together without wanting to tell their spouses. I don't even know how much good it would do. I know Houston would want down hard concrete facts and other than me seeing them and my dad telling me they don't know; I don't have any facts.

My mother is another topic. I don't even know how she would react if I told her. I don't even know if she would care, being she has a secret from my dad. The innocent ones are the boys. They could stand a chance of being brought up in a broken home or a loveless two-parent household. Either way, it isn't fair to them and it's not fair to me. I continued to sit alongside the day bed thinking and thinking. I don't want to hurt them, but they should have thought about their actions.

Suddenly I heard a vehicle crank up. I ran to the living room window and peeped out. It was my dad's old truck. I glanced up at the clock and it was two o'clock. I wonder where he is going this time of morning, but I didn't wonder long. I had a feeling he was seeing Inga. Then I saw the kitchen light come on. I noticed it was my mother. She had sat at the table, and she lit up a cigarette. I smelled it and knew it was one of the ones, I had fixed a few months ago. I thought *she had quit* as I saw her puff away and spray air freshener with each puff.

I made sure not to breathe in the toxic fumes, but she didn't care. *I don't even think she knows I am here because I am half way here anyway* I thought while watching her chain smoke four of them. My dad claims he discarded her smokes while she was in the hospital, but I guess she had them packed away; not even he could find them.

My momma finished smoking, and she went back to bed. I am amazed at how I never noticed how my parents were to each other. Since I been here, they hardly talk. If I am present, they would hold conversation and even eat together but that could be for a show. For the most, my mom had missionary work and my dad would be at the funeral home. I always saw them as in love and so caught up in the things of God.

To me, my mother would be the dictator; while, my dad would always follow orders like a good boy. All of this is very new and hard to grasp. She must think my dad is picking up a body this time of night or maybe he is getting something for her. I went back to the day bed and lay back down. In the morning, I plan to have a chat with my mother even if my dad is around. Daybreak came and I got up. I look outside and my dad was still gone. I washed my face and got changed. I went in the kitchen, and my mother was there. She was sitting at the table as I spoke, "Good morning."

"Good morning."

"Where's dad?"

"He said he's picking up a body last night but when you get here?"

"I came home after the church gathering."

"I didn't know you were here. I swore I was at home alone."

"I slept all night long. I didn't wake up until this morning."

"I got up after your dad left but I went back to bed a little while later."

"Oh ok, where did he go get the body from?"

"I think it was out of town and he won't be back until sometime today."

"I would have gone."

"It's no bother. He's only doing what he's been doing."

"What do you mean?"

"Silly me. He always has dealing with the funeral home. That is what I mean."

"Oh. Ok. I'm about to go. Are you going to be ok alone?"

"Yes. Why wouldn't I?"

"No, reason."

"Get on to work the boys are here."

Inga had the boys. Baker was in her arms sleep while Houston Jr. was in the car seat asleep. They look adorable but not the mother. Inga spoke as she gave my mother the children. I told her to lay Baker in my day bed, and she did. Inga left and I said, "I'm about to go too. See you later."

"Bye Bobby D."

"Bye Mom."

I left her alone with the boys as I went to the car. I got in and drove half a mile. I forgot my money, so I went back to the house. I went in and saw my mother drinking her favorite alcohol and smoking those poisonous cigs. Covering my nose as quickly as I could, I went on in the house. She saw me and said, "What is it?"

"Nothing" I said silently. She still had Houston Jr. in the car seat. I took him out and put him on the other end of the day bed. Baker was still sleep and resting peacefully as I retrieved my money. I tried waiting until she was finished with the cigarette, but she was nowhere near finished. I came out and she was still sitting, smoking and drinking. I almost spoke but she said it for me, "Let me guess? You are displeased with me drinking and smoking."

"You are a grown woman and you been drinking forever. The cigarettes are new so why

would I have an opinion about your life? I am not
the young impressionable lad I used to be. I've
come to terms with a lot of things and a lot of ways
you and dad did, but I am fine with that. It's your
life."

"Everything we ever done was for your
benefit but sometimes you act like you are better
than we are."

"Not better. Just smarter."

She jumped up and ran to the open
room. She came out with Houston Jr. in her arms. I
had a bad feeling as she walked past me and went to
the table. She was speaking as if she were in her
right mind, "I'm about to cut up a baby chicken.
You want some after it comes out the oven?"

I stared at her. In her right hand was the
baby car seat with Houston Jr. in it asleep. She
plopped him on the table. I didn't make any sudden
movement. I don't know how far in left field she is
and I didn't want to find out. I tried encouraging her
by saying, "Mom gives me the baby chicken so I
can cut it up."

"No! Turn the oven on at four hundred and
fifty degrees. You are standing right by it. Hurry up.
I'm starving. I hadn't had a young tender chicken in
a long time."

While walking towards her slowly I stated
happily, "Mom gives me the baby chicken. I can put

onions and seasonings on it. I don't mind helping you cook dad a home cook meal."

When she handed me the baby out the car seat, I rushed to take him back where Baker was. When I came back she was shouting, "Get those things off me! Get them off me Bobby!"

I didn't know what she was talking about. My mom grabbed a knife and was in the process cutting her hand off. I grabbed her by twisting her free arm and hand so she could not cut me or her. My mom was hollering and carrying on about black leaches and worms. I tried soothing her by saying, "They aren't on you now. You cut them all off. Look at your hand. You saved it. You did it all by yourself."

She glanced down at her hand and had a tone of a little child, "I did. I did cut them all off."

Mom kept staring at her hand and arm with amazement; even though, she still had the knife in her hand. I myself, was astounded when I spoke, "Yeah you did so slowly drop the knife, so you won't cut your other hand. You don't want to cut your hand do you, mom?"

"Cut my hand."

"No, mom you don't want to cut your hand. You don't want stitches, do you?"

"No! I don't want stitches. I don't want to cut my hand."

"I don't want you to have them either so drop the knife."

She dropped the knife and I with one quick hit with all my might; I knocked her out. Moments later my dad came home. I told him what happened, and he was just as surprised. He called Inga and told her to come get the boys. She came in a flash and dad was getting on to her for bringing the boys here. She kept telling him she could not afford day care and how they don't have the money. Inga looked at me and said, "Thank you for being here Bobby D. Who knows what would have happened?"

"Thank your God, HE allowed me to double back."

My dad said, "You know I would do anything in the world for you and the boys. All you had to do was ask me for the money and it'll be yours."

Inga sounded as if she was sad when she replied, "I know but Lee, Houston and I can't keep depending on you for help. We must stand on our own sometime. You won't be around always."

"Inga, I'll be around as long as God allows me. I want to help provide for you all. Just tell me what you all need so I can go get it for you; if the need be."

He was all in her face and she was a little nervous. Dad walked closer and must have let it slip his mind that I am in the room watching him being so protective over the boys; who were still asleep. He reached up and touched her face as if he was in love. He must think my eyes are closed and how I am still close by. She lightly kissed his fingers, and he smiled. I made a noise and broke up the embrace. Inga stuttered as if she was trying to think of something. I pretended not to have seen it. My dad knew I was watching as my mother still lay on the floor. He reached in his wallet and gave Inga some money. I said, "Tell Houston I will be a little late. I have to help my dad."

She said okay as she took the kids to day care. We put my mother in her bed. My dad looked at me and said, "We won't breathe a word of this to anyone."

"And why not? She needs help."
"They will think your mother is looney."

"She is beyond looney. What do you think would have happened if I hadn't back tracked?"

"Bobby D., lets' not talk about it."

"Well you should. She smokes and drinks like she is her own person, but her mishaps are hurting us; just like her pressure did to me all those years ago."

"She is just stressed and drinking and smoking helps calm her nerves."

"What about my nerves? I don't do either and neither do you."

"We all are different, and we handle stress differently."

"You are covering for her. Why?"

"I am not covering for her. Your mother is a very important lady and a pillar in the community. She is just having some things going on right now. I believe she will be back on track."

"I doubt she can quit sneaking and smoking; when we are all gone. Like last night you up and left. While you were gone, she got up and chain smoked. I was here and I saw her but the important thing is, where were you?"

He stared at me as if could read his mind. I couldn't and I didn't try. Truth of the matter is, I didn't care where he was or who he was going to see for that matter. He is acting like my mom but on a more discreet level. He is a cheater and just thinking about him and Inga that night, was bothering me. My dad glanced at me and I stared back at him. He must be destined not to answer the question, but he doesn't know who I am and what I do to cheaters. My dad dropped his head, looked away then spoke casually, "Do not breathe a word to anyone about what happened today. Is that clear?"

"What about the beautiful Inga? Won't she tell it since it did involve her children? She might tell her husband, you know your nephew, Houston."

"She won't say a word, and neither will you. Is that understood?"

"I won't say a word but if she comes after me with a knife, I promise you I will embalm her as you plan her funeral."

January
Chapter 14

    Christmas was here and I bought Baker a new bike and some toy Hot Wheel cars. I know little boys love them and I was right. Baker couldn't stop thanking me enough about the toys. Houston Jr. on the other hand, got a few hand-held toys for teething. I even bought a bigger play pen for the boys to get in and or sleep in. I didn't exchange gifts with the others like old times sake, I told them that I was doing something different and I am. They have no idea just how different this coming year is going to be.

    During the whole Christmas dinner, I saw how my dad was handy to my mom. He was on her every beck and call. She went without nothing, and he made sure of that. I even saw how loving Inga was to Houston. It still didn't change my opinion of either of them. My own mother was a gracious host to all those that came by and I like always hid out of sight after showing my face for a few. But today I played with the boys and enjoyed myself. They made me laugh and they made me forget how pushy my childhood was.

    For the first time in a long time, I had a genuine smile on my face. I had no idea how children could do that to an adult. It was like a new world as I played peek-a-boo with Houston Jr. and push toy cars with Baker. This is the childhood I wish I had; one that was happy and one that mattered. This coming year, I plan for my New Year to be a better one as I get my plan into action. This Christian thing is something I was trying but whenever it crossed my mind, I was reminded about the deceit and treachery in my life. I love to do good, but I feel so much better when I do bad to the people that deserve it. I hear people say all the time to let God do it but what if I feel God is using me to do it? I glanced over at my mom, and she smiled.

I gave her a half smile because I don't believe in faking. Although, these people have caused me to do a lot of pretend. However, it was nice seeing my mom was doing a lot better since she smoked all the lethal cigarettes up. She was still drinking and getting drunk. I didn't tell Houston about the voice I heard or what my mom did. Being quiet, makes me feel like a fraud by not telling him what I think he should know about his children. I looked up and Inga walked by my door. It has taken every ounce of good to not say anything to her.

She goes around this place and acts so in love with Houston; at the same time, she is with my dad. I can't stand it. I swear I can't. I tried to be the perfect child, but I find myself being the vigilante. I must give it to Inga, she stays out my way and she seldom speaks. While Houston looks like a fool for being faithful. All he needs to do is act like he wants justice, and I'll do it for free. Whenever they are on bad terms, he will say like he always says, "I put it all in God's hands." I would tell him what if God's hands are full; then what? He'll laugh at me and that would be the end of the conversation. I hate my dearly beloved cousin is being played by the two he trust, the most; other than myself.

But here I am almost thirty and my parents still have me in their clutches; and not in a good way. Above all my dad is the worse. The way he has been doing things has completely opened my eyes about him. He runs around the funeral home like he is the most important person here but he is not. He acts like he is the man in charge when it actuality, it is Houston. My dad even pretends to call the shots about this or that, but he is nothing to me. My heart is growing cold towards him with each passing day.

It's bad enough to not defend your child when the other parent controls with an iron fist but to be a cheater and a weak, pathetic man at that; is by far the worse. He acted like he is God's gift and for a long time, I believed it. I never thought my dad to be as bad as my mom, but he is. He has no idea how

I remember what I did to men and women like him. He would detest the day he got me involved in his lies and dark secrets.

A light came on in my head. I saw the way Inga smiled and gave my dad a nod while she thought no one was looking. I was. I saw their special nod; which meant later or something along those lines. I will see as I time them. Houston came over to me and spoke, "You getting pretty good with the boys. When are you going to get your own?"

"After the way, I see how people call themselves in love do the ones they love; I'm not so sure about that."

"You can't let what others do determine your output on love, Bobby D."

"I'll just say this. I will make sure that person is real with me before I decide on anything and that is pushing it. I've seen how people lie so well to be so happy when they are living a lie. I don't want that."

"You have common fears about love and that is fine. I don't want you to die lonely and broken." I was quiet as Inga came over and said,
"I'm stopping by the baby shower."
Houston looked at his watch and said, "It's late. I'm sure the baby shower is over."

"No. They just called me and told me to come on. Will it be ok if you take the boys on home? I promise I won't be too late coming back."

"Go on sweets and have fun."

They kissed as she left out the house. I didn't say a word. My mom came over and said she was about to call it the night. She gave Houston and me a kiss as she went off to bed. My dad came over and asked, "What are you two about to get into?"

"I am going to bed soon as Houston takes his family home."

"Yeah, it is getting a little late. We all better get going home."

My dad looks at his watch and said, "It's hardly eight. That's not late. You sure you don't want to stay longer?"

"No, Uncle Lee. I'm going home and calling it the night myself."

"What about Inga?"

"She is going by the baby shower then coming on home."

"That baby shower was this evening at seven."

"Yes. It was at the church" Houston added.

I handed him the baby and said my goodnights. Moments later Houston left and so did my dad. He didn't tell me he was going out; not that he had too. I didn't say a word. I went in my open room and lay across the day bed. I wasn't sleepy and I didn't feel like making myself go to sleep. The house was quiet and I did miss the boys. I really had fun today with them and I was glad to be involved in their day. These boys helped me in more ways than they will ever know.

Around ten o'clock. I got up and got some water. My mother was sitting at the table eating pie. She saw me and asked, "You thought I was drinking?"

"When it comes to you, there is no telling what you are doing."

"I'll take that" she said as she took a gulp of her liquor.

I got some water and was headed back to my room, but she stopped me by asking, "Don't you want to come in here and talk to your mother?"

I turned around and said, "No. I don't have anything to say to my mother."

"Don't you want to know about the long nights your dad takes when he thinks I am sleep or when you are not here?"

She had my full attention as I paced myself back to her slowly. She gave me that sneaky smile when she spoke, "Now that got your attention."

I sat down across from her and said, "What he does or where he goes has nothing to do with me."

Mother took a shot of liquor and said, "I'm waiting. Go on and ask me."

"Ask you what? I told you it's none of my business what he does or where he goes but you seem to know all the answers to the questions you ask. So why don't you tell me."

"You are the one who holds secrets better than anyone. Come on out and tell me because I know you know."

"Know what mother?" I questioned because I wasn't going to let her coheres me into saying something I did not. I've seen her do it too many times to people, but I am not those people.

"Since you act like this is my first rodeo, you must now be just finding out or you been known?"

"Know what?" I asked in a coy way.

"About your dad and Inga, what else?" I was stunned as she said it calmly with a swallow of liquor. I asked, "Dad and Inga?"

"Yes. Houston is the only one that doesn't know. He is so immature when it comes to life other than God. He doesn't have a clue that his dear sweet uncle has been going with his gorgeous wife for years."

"For years?"

"Yes. They have been going together for years" she said so calmly.

"Mom maybe you are delusional and don't know what you are talking about."

"You hope I am delusional but trust me, I am as sober as you think. Inga and Lee started seeing each other right after you left."

"Why haven't you said anything if you knew all this time?"

"Say something for what? He thinks he is doing something. She makes him feel alive and I don't have to play like I want his, God awful sex. If he wants Inga, then by all means let him have his way with her."

"It's true. It's really true" I kept saying to throw her off if I knew of not.

"How can I not know? Their departures are noticeable, and he has a hint of her cheap perfume when he comes home. Besides I like the way you were trying to see if I really knew what I was talking about before you said anything."
I acted like I didn't hear her as I questioned in a dumb way again, "And you ok with these things you are telling me that is going on?"

"There are a lot of things I know that goes on in this house and I promise you they will come to a head. As for your father, he is smitten with her."

"And it doesn't bother you? The great and powerful Gloria Reed has a husband who sleeps with his nephew's wife?"

"As long as he takes care of me and do not shame me; that's him. He will account for his own sins like we all must do. He can run around with her all he wants. Lee is not going to leave me for her and that I am willing to take to the bank; even on a Sunday."

"Then why hurt Houston? He seems to be the only person in all of this mess that is innocent and doesn't deserve the way all of you are hiding things from him."

"He has the Holy Spirit in him. All he has to do is enquire that of the Lord and HE will show Houston the type of slut he married."

"So, now she is a slut?"

"She has always been that" Mother spoke with authority.

I sat back and watched her drink more and more of her brown then white liquor. Mother said, "When you left your dad was beside himself with guilt. He felt like he could have done something to stop you from living but in truth; there was nothing either one of us could do. You were destined to leave and leaving might have been your calling. Now leaving to do what I don't know but I do know that we wanted your calling to be a spiritual one and one that would lead God's people, but it isn't. You will never be a preacher, as long as the devil is the God of this world. However, only you can choose what it is you want. As your fate plays out before you, mind you I am a lot of things, and probably then some but the Lord still uses me and I still see in the spirit."

"If you see in the spirit then you need to take off your old eyes and put on a pair of new ones. Mother no harm but you see in the spirit is like God saying it's ok to drink and smoke."

Mother laughed at me and said; "Only time will tell if what I see is right or not."

"What does trying to call me out has to do with you and dad?"

"It has everything. You are a keeper of secrets, and you know too much Bobby D."

"What made you think I knew?"

"I know you happen to be around when anyone needs someone to talk too. I also know Mother Clark told you something before she abruptly died."

"You tell me since you know it all."

She poured herself some more liquor as she replied, "I know my friend had help dying."
I didn't say a word. I wasn't letting on I was some of the reason why her friend was dead. I know my mother and I know she is staring at me for some answers; I wasn't going to give her. I smiled when I responded, "So what if she died while I was there."

She lifted her glass in the air as to toast me when she replied, "Oh you were more than just there you have a share in it. Cheers."

Mother drunk some of her liquor then put the glass back on the table. I kept looking as she said, "You might as well go on and tell me. You have people thinking I am looney, and you did a good job with that. You even laced my cigarettes with your precious formaldehyde or was it sodium citrate?"

Mother took a sip of her liquor again and placed the glass on the table again to say, "You didn't think I would know! You; as smart as you are, didn't think I would know what you had been doing to me!"

"Tell me why would I do that to you?" I asked in an even tone.

"The question is why do you think I made you the way you are?"

I spoke as if I was up for an election. She sat there waiting on my answer. I stated, "I didn't realize how much I hated you until I came back home. I didn't realize how much I hated the call of God on my life until I saw you. You are the reason why I do the things I've did. You have pushed me so far down the wrong path that going back is not a possibility. In the beginning, I did have a change of heart but that night I caught my dad and Inga at the funeral home; that changed for me. I never knew of his indiscretion. I esteemed him higher than you but he made you look like an innocent lamb before the slaughter."

226

She sat up some in her chair as she asked, "That's the first time you knew about them?"

"Yes."

"You didn't know whenever he left in the middle of the night, they would meet up at the funeral home. Think about it." With more life she spoke, "Who would come to a funeral home in the middle of the night? No one. The business was their meeting place until you saw them, but she didn't see you and he didn't tell her."

Now it made sense why she would walk around me like nothing was wrong. My dad didn't have the heart to tell his young interest, how his child caught them together. Mother said, "Who is stealing the funeral home money? I know Houston has called you here to help uncover the thief."

"He wanted me here to help with the business too, but you seemed to already know, don't you?"

"Mother Clark and I were doing some investigations of our own. She told you what she thought before she had help dying. But the kicker is she was telling the enemy the whole time. You aren't the one stealing the money, but I would have loved to have seen her face when you killed her."

"I didn't" was all I said as my mother stated, "I have you on tape. Her whole house was under surveillance. I saw you hit her. The punch made her heart malfunction."

I sat there and she said with a slight smile, "You can't deny it but the added touch was what you said to her about the man raping the girls and fucking the boys. That was a hell-of a thing to say to an old woman that was about to die and see Jesus."

"I say what I think. I got that from you mother."

She poured some more liquor as she said, "I am not going to turn it in if that is what you want to know."

"It isn't and I don't care. About time they could indict me, I'll be gone like the wind."

"Don't worry I destroyed it but I had to let you know, I know all about your evil ways."

I looked away to say, "I had just pleaded with God to make me over. I had cried and when I finished crying, I felt better to only see what I saw."

I was getting angrier by the second. She broke my concentration when she spoke with laughter, "You wonder why I am not mad at you for doing what you have done to me? Bobby D. you ruined my career, and you made me look stupid to the church. You come back home with an agenda, and you think I am going to let it ride."

"I don't know or care what you do. You can't stop me if hurting you is what I want to do."

"No, I can't stop you but rests assure I have a plan as well."

"You can't fight the flies off your ass, mother."

"The next time you lift your hand to hit me, you better make sure I don't get up again."

"I assure you when I lift these hands up at you again, you won't get up again."

I got up and walked off from her.

February
Chapter 15

For the entire month of January and up until now; the last day of February my mother and I didn't speak. She knows I had something to do with Mother Clark but other than the hit she doesn't know. Something is telling me I need to hurry up leave. I got to work and saw Houston. He was happy as I asked him, "What has you so happy?"

"Inga is having a baby. My Inga is having a baby."

"She is?"

"Yes, and I hope this one is our little girl."

I almost asked him if it was his but refrained as I saw my dad. He was coming out his office as I yelled out, "Dad."

He stopped and came over. I was watching my dad for any sudden facial features or body movements as Houston said, "Uncle Lee, my Inga has done it again."

"What has she done?"

"She is having a baby. She is having a baby."

My dad looked like he had seen a dead man walking as he came back to reality with the words, "Congrats Houston. I am so proud of you both. When is it due?"

"June."

I calculated in my head and that was right around the time she was with my dad here in the sleeping room. To rub salt in my dad's wound I said with joy to Houston, "Aren't you lucky to have such a faithful wife?"

"I am Bobby D."

"Dad, isn't he blessed to have a wonderful and faithful wife as Inga?"

"Houston is beyond blessed and her having a baby is wonderful."

"Where is she at now?" I asked.

"She is in her office."

My dad said, "Let me go in and congratulate her first."

He walked off from us and Houston said, "Let me get back to work. We have another funeral to do on Saturday. Have you embalmed the body yet?"

"I did that yesterday."

"Ok. I forgot who I was asking."

Houston went back to his office, and I went towards Inga. I only caught the cat by the tail as I heard him say, "A baby, huh?"

I accidentally bumped the door, and they changed the conversation to a happier on by saying how happy and excited she was of her and Houston. I went on and knocked on the door; then the phone rang. Inga answered it as I stood in the door frame. She waved and said, "It's your mother."

My dad looked at me and I asked, "Who she wants?"

"She wants to talk to you Bobby D."

Inga handed me the phone, and I purposely hung up but pretended she was on the phone as I said, "Hello. Hello."

They looked at me as I said, "Dad we might need to go check on her."

"Yeah, we better go on and do that."

Inga said, "You two go on. Houston and I are leaving for the day. We going to the Health Department."

I smiled as I walked out first. Dad came behind me and we walked down the hall to my little room. I said, "If you don't mind can you go to your office and bring me the new policy, I want to go over it."

"What about your mom?"

"I'm going to call her and tell her we will be a few minutes late."

He turned right around, and I got on my cell and called my mother. She picked up as I was fixing the chlorine chloroform. I told her we would be a little late and she wondered what I was talking about. I explained how we got disconnected. I rushed her off so I can get dad. The towel was soaked with the chloroform as I waited behind the door. Luckily, he is a small like man and knocking him out would not be a problem. Soon as he opened the door he said, "I didn't see it."

Hurriedly I covered his mouth and nose. He was struggling with me but he was no match for me. I overpowered him as we both went to the floor. I continued to hold him for about five minutes as he laid in my arms out cold. I got up and picked him up. I put him on the table and strapped him down and put an IV in his neck. He was out for about thirty minutes. I took his shoes off and gave his bare feet a slight tap. He moved his head side to side as I spoke softly, "Oh dad. Wake up."

He was groggy as he moaned. I said it again, "Oh dad. Wake up. It's time for us to have that talk."

He tried moving but he saw that he could not move. I sat on the roller chair facing him. His voice was low and with groggy words but I heard him say, "What's going on?"

"Nothing for now. I want us to have that talk and you being honest depends on you getting up- alive."

In a clearer tone he asked, "What you want to know?"

"Tell me from the beginning about you and Inga."

He was silent before he the words that came out of his mouth were, "When you left, she comforted me and one thing led to another."

"Did any of those roads lead you to doing the right thing?"

"No."

"What about the baby she carries? Is it yours?" I asked to see if he could produce more children.

"I believe so" I spoke with a faint smile of joy.

"How do you believe that?"

"Houston's sperm count is zero."

"What?" I said faintly.

He turned he head as to make up his mind about what to tell me. I asked, "Go on and tell me!"

"Houston can't create children. I know it and Inga knows it."

"How did you know it?"

"Houston got sick, and the doctor told Inga. She told the doctor she will tell him, but she told me. She never told him. That is when we first found out Baker was not his. She and I did a blood test on Houston Lee and he too is mine."

I was silent as I asked, "Houston doesn't know does he?"

My dad didn't say a word. I yelled in his face as I spit on him, "Answer me!"

"No, he doesn't know. If Inga had told him then he would wonder who the father of the boys was."

"You don't think he has the right to know! You don't think he should know about the trickery his wife and favorite uncle has done!" My dad was quiet as he said in a cracked voice, "He has the right to know but God I don't know how we would tell him. It is easier for him to pretend the children are his than to break his heart by telling him those little boys, he loves are not. There was no other way. You have to believe me."

He cried. I have never seen my dad cry, but hatred and evil made me say, "No sense of crying. You should have thought about all that when you messed off with your nephew's wife."
Dad said a little plainer, "Do you know Houston is your brother?"
If mom hadn't told me, I would have been shocked as I said, "Yeah, your wife told me. Did you know she knows about you and Inga? She knows all about the nights you spend with your lovely niece in law."

His head faced me in a quick motion. I spoke, "Yes. Your wife knows about you and Inga. She told me all about it. I acted like I didn't know but she knew I knew. She says I keep everybody's secret and quite naturally, I would have your secret too."

"Are you going to let me up?" he asked as if it were all over.

To keep him wondering of his fate I spoke in a confused manner, "I don't know yet? I'm still waiting on you to come clean and tell me everything I need to know.'

He didn't say a word and neither did it for a few moments. Finally, I stated plainly, "Yeah. I guess me knowing determines your fate."

I got up and walked around. He watched me as I came back to him. I sat down and asked, "Why have you been stealing from the business?"

"I was doing it for the boy's future. I was making sure they were taking care of. I don't think Houston would want the boys if he knew the truth. I was planning on leaving your mother and she was leaving him. We were going to take our children and leave town. I love her and I know Inga loves me just as much."

I stared at him as my heart became freezing at fifty degrees below zero. I opened the artery and his blood started draining. He spoke, "I told you the truth about everything. Please don't do this to me. I want to raise my boys and grow old with the woman I love."

With no answer, I watch his blood drain more and more as I said, "I esteemed you higher

than mom, but I found out you are worse than her.
At least she never cheated."
He was trying to talk but the draining of his
blood made him weak. I said, "You don't know
how I despise liars, cheaters and sin. Just for that I
am draining your body of seven pints of blood.
That'll be just enough for you not to feel your legs
and arms. You know you'll be unconscious, right?"

"Bobby D. don't do this. I love you."

"And I loved you too, dad" I spoke with ice in
my tone.

My dad was fighting it but he and I both
know, it takes the body time to rebuild lost blood.
At this point, he has no way of rebuilding it.
He tried lifting himself but couldn't. I saw I was
close to seven pints. He rolled his head and became
unconscious. I waited until I got the seven pints
and took the IV out his neck. I unstrapped
him, picked him up and carried him outside.

When I opened the outside door to
the crematoria furnace, I laid him on the floor and
opened the cast iron door. I rolled out the iron bed
and picked him up. I placed him feet first and
closed the door. I didn't even turn it on to preheat.
Once I locked the outside of the iron bed, the
heat came rapidly. I sat there and watched as my
dad slowly became aware of what was happening.

He is too weak to fight; even if he could, he couldn't bust out.

He rolled his neck back and saw me from outside of the heated door. He lifted his hands as to pray but the fire quickly engulfs him. I didn't feel sorry for him cheating. I didn't feel bad for killing him. I looked at it as a business. I was sent here to clean up and that is what I plan to do. I watched my dad being burned alive and I am unbothered by it. To me he was another job that a client sent for me to do and I did it to perfection. I put his burned body on the back burner. When he was just a heap of ashes, I took them without cooling.

I placed him in a dustpan and began reciting Psalm 23 as I spread him all over the business grounds; since he loves this place so much. I made up my mind to do what the cowards in this family wouldn't do. After watching my dad being blown around, I went to Houston's house. Inga's car was gone. I was glad but Houston was there. I got out with many things on my mind. I was concerned as to where the boys were. When Houston saw me I asked, "You guys back from the Health Department so soon?"

"Yeah, Inga got sick, and I told her we can go tomorrow."

"Where are the boys?"

"They were worn out from playing today at the park. I brought them back home, fed them and put them to bed so I can have some peace and quiet."

"Where's Inga now?"

"When she got to feeling better, she went to do a little shopping. What's up?"

"Houston, we have a few things to discuss and I don't know how you will take it."

"You have me nervous Bobby D."

"I am the one nervous because I have things to tell you that no one in this family has the courage to."

"You have my curiosity peeked."

"Will the boys be ok if we go outside to your back yard?"

"Yes, they will be fine."

I followed him out to the back patio. We sat down as I said, "I have a few bombs to drop and I don't know which of the ones is the lesser."

"Just pick a bomb and blow away."

Not knowing which one was the less, I made up my mind when I spoke, "My mother says I keeps everyone's secret and that is why I think you should hear it all from me; since I know them all."

"I'm listening."

"My mom told me you are my brother and not my cousin."

He stared at me with many questions on his face. I know what he is thinking so I said, "She told me she and your dad; Uncle Paul were together. She said she didn't know he was married but found out later. She says your mom Marie was sterile, but she told your dad she was pregnant when in fact my mom was pregnant with you. After my mom gave birth to you, she said she let your mom Marie pretend to be the mother while your dad was away in the military. While your dad was away, Aunt Marie died, and she told your dad that your mom left the baby with her. My mom said she changed her life and went overseas and that is when she met my dad; you're Uncle Lee. She said she didn't know they were brothers until it was too late. When your dad Uncle Paul started blaming you, she encouraged him to let you stay with us and that is the real reason why you came to live with us. She wanted you with her."

Houston said slowly, "All my life I was taught that my mom died because of me. The whole time my real mom lived. All my life my dad blamed me for something I didn't do."

"Yes."

Houston got up and I got up with him. He said angrily, "Why didn't she tell me? She has told me everything else, but she failed to tell me the most important thing in my life."

"I guess she had lived with the lie so long and thought why change it now after all these years."

Houston said, "I know now how to some degree I favored her. I didn't think it was possible to favor an aunt that isn't really in your family but it's because she is my real mom."

"Houston, I am sorry for having to tell you these things. Are you going to ask her?"

"No. If she wanted me to know she would have told me. She wanted to keep it a secret so I will be one to keep her secret."

"Don't you want to know why?"

He glanced at me and said, "I do want to know but if she didn't want to tell me."

I was quiet as I said, "You need to embrace yourself then."

"What more is it?"

"A little more."

By him asking me that; makes the rest of what I to tell him even harder. Never in my life had I thought that telling him what I have too would be like this. It is in fact, harder once I look at it but I know I can't turn back. I said you might need to sit down for the rest of this. He watched me like a homeless child. He sat down and put his head on my shoulder. I said, "Your sperm count is so low, that a lift by God is the only thing that can bring it up."

"What are you talking about? How you know about a sperm count of mine?"

"My dad told me."

"How did he know, if I don't know?"

"Inga told him when she found out."

"But how is that when we have two boys and one on the way."

I was quiet as it hit him. He jumped up and stared at me as if he was hit by something as he questioned, "Those aren't my boys?"

I was quiet again. Houston started crying and saying, "Oh God! Not my boys please! Don't say that Bobby D.! Take it back! Please take it back! Don't tell me those two; I love with all my heart; are not mines!"

He watched me to see if I would retract what I said. I didn't. Houston laid his head on me and cried harder and harder. I pat his back and said, "Let it out. I am here for you."

Houston cried for like hours. He lifted up his head to ask, "Who is the daddy? Who did my Inga sleep with to get my boys?"

Not having a clue how to break it down I said, "Sure you want to know that? It's already hard enough to tell you what I have so far."

"Bobby D. I desire to know who is the man my wife cheated with, to father MY BOY'S."

Taking a deep breath, I said, "My dad."

It must have registered his brain. Houston gave me a look as if all the wind had been knocked out of him as he whispered gently, "Uncle Lee?"

"Yes, Uncle Lee" I spoke as I studied his face.

"You mean, my uncle that works hand in hand with me in this business? The same one that told me he has it in his will for me to have?"

"Houston, that night on Halloween I gave my life back to God. I went in the funeral home and caught them in my sleeping room. She didn't see me, but my dad did. It hurts me more than you think and for what it's worth, I felt like you had the right to know; just who you say you love and how people will take the love you have for them and not care about it until it's too late."

Houston cried as he stated, "You sure you saw what you saw?"

"She was on top of him riding him and he had his hands on her hips. How can I mistake that? Besides, he confessed how they been together ever since I left. My dad says she was comforting him and one thing led to another."

"They been sleeping around under my nose all these years and I didn't have a clue?"

"They would meet up at the funeral home." My brother dropped his head in a shameful way. I tried to encourage him when I said, "It is not your fault she cheated, and he deceived you."

"But under my nose, Bobby D. under my nose. I should have seen or known something because for the last eight years it was mainly the three of us. We had part-time workers but not long enough to come in and stay. There were times, they went on business trips or went on long journeys together that I could not make. And all those times, my uncle was making love to my faithful wife."

"Yeah, but you won't have to ever worry about my dad sneaking around with your wife again" I added softly.

"Why is that?"

"He has spread himself too thin, sort of speak."

"I don't care to ever know where he's at." For about five minutes, Houston sat with his head down. He shook his head up and down as he asked, "I guess he was the one stealing from the business?"

"Yes. He told me he was stealing from business because of the boys. He didn't think you would want them after you found out they weren't yours."

"My wife and my uncle? Bobby, why they do this to me? I love those boys and to think they are not mine hurts me almost as their treachery" Houston spoke as he hit his chest really hard numerous of times.

My cousin, my brother held his stomach as he cried. He is broken and full of all kinds of emotions. I know he is hurting because of the pain that is gripping him. I stated silently, "I know it hurts but you can get better. I know you can because of your faith. You can heal and go on. You have more faith in the love and power of Jesus than anyone I know. Don't let this make you like it made me."

Tears were all over him as his body shook from the pain. He lifted his head up for a second to ask, "Do they know you are telling me? Do those two know you are telling me all of this? Does our mother know you know all of this?"

"She knows I know. As for Inga and my dad, no I took it upon myself to tell you. I want you to know because I am tired of being the one who holds all the secrets of others."

Houston dropped his head back down and sat there while crying. I could only pat his back as he used my shoulder to cry on. He didn't deserve the way my parents and his wife has done him. Houston always did right and to think he is the victim hurts me more. I don't know how long he and I sat in his back yard, and I didn't care. He needed me as a friend, and I was not going to let him down. My brother stopped crying as he heard Inga's car pull up. I asked, "Are you going to tell her that you know?"

"I am going to show her that I know."

"You want me to leave?"

"No, Bobby D. I think you need to stay in case I can't stop myself."

Chapter 16

Houston got up and stormed towards the house. The closer he got to her he slowed his pace down. He stood there and stared at his wife. They have been together for so many years and been through a lot in those years. I don't know how it feels to be with someone for so long just to find out they were untrue to you. My brother has a lot of feelings rushing him and I know he is trying to control them but when you are faced with reality, controlling yourself is the last thing that comes to mind.

He wants to make them pay and I believe they should; even if children are involved. She got out the car and he kind of dropped his head and shoulders. I knew he was making sure she didn't see a clear picture of his face. I caught up with Houston as Inga looked up and spoke, "Oh hey Bobby D. what brings you out here at ten o'clock at night?"

I didn't get a chance to answer as he spoke for me, "Bobby D. is here to see me."

"Oh. Ok. Houston, are you going to help your pregnant wife or keep standing there while I hold get all these heavy bags?"

For a split second, Houston stood there. I started helping her. He snapped out of Hurtvilleand helped her. Inga opened the back door as we all went inside. I went to the boy's room, and they were still asleep. I closed the door softly and went back to the kitchen. Inga was going on and on about her shopping experience and how her feet ached. She didn't notice how her husband was extremely without words until I said, "Are you ok? You seem distant tonight."

"I'll be okay," Houston said with things on his mind.

Sounding sexy Inga said, "I have something that will bring you back home when your company leaves."

He didn't say a word. She glanced over at me. Inga smiled and asked, "Can you take these upstairs, while Bobby D. leaves?"

"Yeah, let me get these upstairs."

He took a few bags and left the room. I said, "Inga."

"Yes, Bobby D. It's time for you to go home. I want to spend the rest of this night with my husband."

She stopped talking for she saw something behind me as she shouted, "Please don't hurt him! Please don't hurt our son!"

My body did a jolt spin. I saw Houston with a Houston Jr. in one hand and a knife in the other. He placed the knife near the baby as he spoke calmly, "Inga moves from behind Bobby D. before I kill Houston Jr."

"Whoa Houston put it down before you hurt someone."

He lifted the knife to the boy's throat and pressed some. I knew he was for real as I said, "Houston she is going to move away from behind me so we all can talk about whatever it is that is bothering you."

Inga never spoke a word. Her tears kept her from saying a word. Houston almost screamed, "Shut up Inga and move. I will not tell you again."

This time she moved out the way with her hands up as if she was surrendering. Houston said, "I'm will ask you some questions and you telling me the truth is important; is that understood?"

Crying in her voice, Inga replied "Yes. I will answer you."

"Are you sleeping with my Uncle Lee?"

Inga cried for her life. I stood by and watched. To me, that is why I never liked secrets. That word secret, has a way of biting you when you least expect it. That one word has destroyed many lives and many relationships has been lost because of it. I noticed how Houston was doing the best he can to control his pain. I saw how Inga was avoiding his pain but when you lie and sin; your secrets will find you out. I hate this has happened to them because I have loved these two forever. I just wish they all would have stayed clean but sin is a dirty business and it never comes out clean.

I moved over some so he could have a clear view of Inga. Her eyes were puffy as her husband spoke impatiently, "I will not wait again on your answer. Are you sleeping with my Uncle Lee?"

"I was. I told him I couldn't leave with him because I loved you more."

"What you mean by leave?"

"I was taking the children and leaving you. He was leaving his wife. I told him I couldn't do it but I loved you more. He said he understood."

I knew she was lying. I cut my eye at her, and she ignored me. Houston said, "Is she telling the truth Bobby D.?"

Before I could answer she said, "What would Bobby D. know?"

"She is lying" I spoke out.

"Bobby D. no! Please Bobby D. don't do this to me and my children."

I ignored her pleas with these words, "She is lying. Her and my dad planned on running away from you both."

"Bobby D. why are you doing this to me?"

"You did it to yourself. I hate sin and cheaters and liars are the top of my list. You go to church, and you still cheat and lie to your husband. You have been with Houston for as long as I could remember and YOU MESSED THAT UP! Not me. Please if you are going to blame someone, start with you and your decisions."

She cried. I felt almost sorry for her. She is a nice person, but we are called to live a Holy life not a good life or a nice life. We are called to fashion ourselves like Christ and not our flesh but that is the problem many people face. They don't want Christ until it is too late, hear bad news or need something from Jesus. Houston spoke, "I believe you Bobby D. You have been the only person that has been honest with me throughout my whole life. I thank you for that. Now back to you Inga, Is this my son?"

Crying again, Inga did not answer as he said, "If you don't think I won't kill him you are wrong. I will kill all of us. Right here! Right now! Answer me! Is- this-my-son?"

"No, Houston he's not yours" Inga spoke with many tears.

As if he was hearing it all over again, Houston tears strolled down his cheeks. He asked, "Is Baker mine?"

Inga was breathing hard as she replied, "No, he is not yours; oh God Houston they aren't yours. The boys aren't yours."

He nodded to her and asked, "What about the one you carry? Is that one even mine?"

She sniffled as she said, "Give me my baby Houston. Please don't hurt him. He has nothing to do with all of this."

"Answer the question. Is that my baby you carry?" Houston shouted.

"No. Houston the children are not yours. Oh God, none of them are yours. I'm so sorry. I'm so sorry. Please forgive me. Please find it in your heart to forgive me."

As if he had heard something in his head Houston said, "Which is more important to you? Your life or the life of Houston Jr.?"

My ears must have heard wrong. Houston is a preacher but a man first. He is asking who is more important to a mother. She stated with loud tears, "Please don't make me choose."

"If you can't choose, I will choose for you and trust me you don't want me to choose."

He was waiting on her to make up her mind as he stated again, "Inga, I loved you with all my heart. I never thought you would do me like this. I gave you everything I had and then some."

"You couldn't take care of me! You couldn't take care of us" she shouted.

"If dear old Uncle Lee wasn't stealing from the business, I could have. You knew I had taken pay cut after pay cut, just to keep things a float, but you didn't care."

"Oh yes, I did Houston" Inga stated as she was trying to clear her face up.

"No! Don't you dare stand there trying to fool me. You can't do it anymore! The entire time I was doing all I can to take care of my family, my uncle was taking care of his family."

"Houston don't think of that. He is the past."

"I know he is the past but right now he is not important. I asked you a question and you need to answer it."

He pushed a little harder on Houston Jr.'s throat and he squirmed a little. He did that to show her he really has the knife on the baby. Inga called out, "His life is more important that mine!"

Houston was quiet, and I was anxious to see where he is going with this. He nodded his head and stated, "Very slowly walk in front of me to our bedroom."
Inga was sniffing and shaking as she walked in front of Houston and the baby. I was standing there as Houston called out, "You too Bobby D."

I walked in a fast pace to catch up with them. We all walked upstairs, and Inga pushed open the bedroom door. I thought she would hit him or something, but she didn't. I know that is what I would have done. I would not keep walking and not do anything, but she did. The four of us went in the room and Houston said, "Very slowly pull out the forty-five gun, from the dresser drawer."

She cried and saying, "Bobby D. tell Houston to let us go. I beg you."

"Shut your lying tongue up! Your voice irritates me and to hear you speak makes me sick. Now shut up and get the gun slowly. If you try anything I will kill Houston Jr. without thinking." Inga got the gun out and tried handing it to him, but he said, "No. Put the gun to your head and pull the trigger."
I was blown away. I know he wouldn't listen, and I didn't care if he did nor not. I was on his side because of the pain that was done. I knew he is caught up and her pulling the trigger was a good idea. By her doing this, he didn't touch her and no prosecutor could convict him or put the gun in his hand. That was really a smart idea. Inga was nervous. I wanted her to hear before she died that someone was on her side. I am going to lie to her like she lied to him. I tried defending her when I said, "Houston, just let her and the children go. You have no ties to them. Surely you aren't going to let this woman kill herself in front of her child."

"He won't remember anything; just like I won't remember anything. I will say I was

254

downstairs and I heard a gunshot. I came upstairs and found my lovely pregnant wife dead."

He has all of this mapped out, I thought. I replied, "What about the baby in her stomach?"

"What about it? It's not mine."

Inga cried as he stated, "Put the gun to your head and kill yourself. If you don't I promise you, the boys will die tonight."

Inga said, "Tell my boys I love them and I would have done anything for them."

"I won't tell them those lies."

Inga cried as I said, "I will tell them for you."

She looked over at me and put the gun to her head. I thought he was going to stop her but he didn't. In a blink of an eye, Inga had pulled the trigger and killed herself. Her soul was gone, just like that. Blood splatted all over the spot and bed. Little Houston Jr. shook some but he did not wake up. Houston cried and cried. I walked over to her and checked her pulse. She was a fighter and still breathing. I leaned near to say, "I would never tell those boys that for you. Tell my daddy hello when you see him in Hell."

Inga turned her head towards my voice. I said, "That's right. I just burned him alive for his cheating ways."

I can tell she was trying to say something. I laughed at her. Inga's body shook as she stopped breathing. Houston threw the knife down as he held onto Houston Jr. for dear life. I got up and said, "She's gone."

"Oh Bobby D. what have I done? What have I done!"

"You haven't done anything. You are innocent and you will be ok."
Houston was hysterical and crying. I stated, "Calm down and let me get rid of the body for you."
He stared up at me and cried as he said, "No. She killed herself and I will call the police. You go on home, and we will talk later."

"Houston, I love you. I have always loved you like a brother and to know you are really my brother makes me love you more. I will not tell what transpired tonight. She killed herself and that was her fault. I will never tell your secret."
I gave him a hug.

March
Chapter 17

It's a little after midnight and it's the first day of March. This is the month I am leaving and never coming back to this place. I am cutting all ties with my mother and everybody. I believe I have helped the business, and my time here is up. I went to the funeral home and packed a few of my things. I called a taxi and told them to pick me up in an hour. I got in the hearse and went towards my parent's home. There are few things I need to get there. *Leave them* I heard my mind say but I kept driving. When I pulled up in the driveway, the lights were off. *Good, she's asleep* I thought.

I opened the back door, and she flicked on the living room light. *What now?* I thought as she said, "Come in here for a minute Bobby D. before you rush off."
I sighed and walked in the living room. She was sitting in her favorite recliner chair with a blanket pulled up to her breast. She made me feel uncomfortable, but I can take her out if the need be. I already took out my dear old dad. I walked in and said, "What do you want this time of night? Shouldn't you be sleep?"

"I should be asleep, but I couldn't."

"Why can't you not sleep?"

"I had a dream you killed your father."

"Wow those cigarettes gave you those dreams?" I said to insult her.

"No. I still pray to God. How else did you think I found out about what you were doing to me?"

"I don't know. The house has hidden cameras."

She sat up some as she asked, "Have you killed your dear old dad?"

I didn't answer her. She said, "You really don't have to answer because I found out all about your freelance lifestyle. I know all about how you make people pay for doing sins."

"And how you know that mother?"

"I had someone to track you down. I must admit you weren't an easy find. You disappeared off the map and you call yourself doing things in the name of Jesus. You honestly believe you are going to go to heaven because you get hired to humiliate people."

"I didn't say that you did."

She was quiet as I said, "I may not be perfect, but I know how you made me feel. I know how you helped push me so far from God that it made no sense how I felt over the years."

"Is it because of me or you? Now you do know that you are not to follow man for we are flesh and blood. You know it is up to you to find out for yourself about God and how HE is real in your life. I do say I was not the best example, but regardless you must find your own way and if you chose not to serve Jesus that is on you. I may have pushed you but when you got grown the walk became all yours."

I yelled at her, "YOU DON'T THINK YOUR PUSH, PUSHED ME OVER THE EDGE!"

She was smug when she replied, "No. I showed you the right way and you choose the way you wanted so don't blame this all on me. You are just as guilty of the way you turned out. If you didn't want to live right that was your call. Now I ask, have you already killed your father?"

"Yes, I murdered the cheating bastard. Do I need to get rid of you?"

She smiled an evil smile when she responded, "That has been the problem the whole time. I allowed your dad to call you Bobby D. We should have been calling you by your real name, Bobbiana Delyn Reed."

Getting closer to her so I could position myself to hit her, I sounded almost like a five-year old when I called out, "Didn't I tell you to call me Bobby."

I dropped my head because I haven't heard my real name in a long time. My mother sat up some more. She spoke as to get under my skin, "You have a beautiful name but an evil heart Bobbiana Delyn."

Lifting my head slowly, I stared into her cruel malicious face. She had that cocky appeal about her. I gathered my thoughts to say, "I know how beautiful you will look embalmed-alive."

"You don't have that much heart" mother said to taunt me.

"Mother, I will snatch your skeleton out your body and watch your skin do a meltdown."

Being my mother and having her assertiveness attitude she responded back even colder, "The day you do, is the day you are through. Don't try to be a bitch, be THE BITCH! I guarantee your feet can't walk in my shoes."

I smiled back at her and casually proclaimed, "I'll do better than that. I'll half embalm you and bury you face down; so, you can say hello to Hell, as we kiss your ass goodbye."

"I'll haunt you every day for the rest of your lonely, miserable pathetic life."

"Too bad, I don't believe in ghost."

Before I could grab her, she pulled out a revolver and shot me in the center of my chest right near my heart. I staggered back and looked at her. I glanced down and lifted my hand up to feel the blood oozing out of me. I even tasted the blood. My body was getting weak as I fell to my knees. My mother got up and I fell over. I was closing my eyes as I heard her say, "I be damned if I go to jail because of your evil ass."

Chapter 18

      I didn't hear the sound of angels singing as my eyes opened slowly. Some say if you go to heaven the angels will sing for you but today that was not the case. I opened my eyes and tried moving my arms. I looked down and saw I was chained to this wall and not only that, I could see straight through my body.

      I had put on a spiritual body. You know the one that never burns. The one you will have throughout eternity. I panicked as I heard people hollering and crying. I even heard voices of people praying and begging the Lord to forgive them and to give them another chance. I even heard the imps of Satan laughing as they proclaimed, "There is no way out. You are here because you didn't live Holy so shut up and burn up."

      I'm in Hell. The Abyss. The Bottomless Pit. The Underworld. I am really here with no way out. I know people say it is not real, but it is real. This place does exist and I hate I didn't live the life I should have. I wanted to repent and have my life be a do over, but I know that does not happen. I know the Lord has mercy on who HE will, but if I had known I was taking a chance by living without HIM, I might have changed the way I felt or the way I did things. I am stuck here in this place forever with only the memories, apologies, should have's, could have's and would have's.

Please live right and don't wait until it is too late to serve the Lord Jesus. Do it while you still have breath in your body. It doesn't matter how much education, money, connections, theories, or excuses you have; you will go to a grave of six feet deep if not cremated. Run for Christ while you are still on top of the ground with blood running warm in your veins. Don't do like I did and like many others that allowed how we felt about things to consume us. Even holding a grudge, not willing to let go or not forgiving can halter and hinder your salvation.

I know people say nothing is written in stone but if you go to Hell, there is no way out and that is written in the Word of God; which is the stone.

"DON'T LIVE IN HELL THEN DIE AND GO TO HELL, FOREVER."

Epilogue

Houston kept the children. He sold the funeral home. After the funerals of his mother and sister, he moved away to an unknown place.

Houston was never charged with the murder of his wife. The DA saw it as a suicide.

They never knew or found the remains of Lee Reed.